IRON MAN

IRON ARMORY

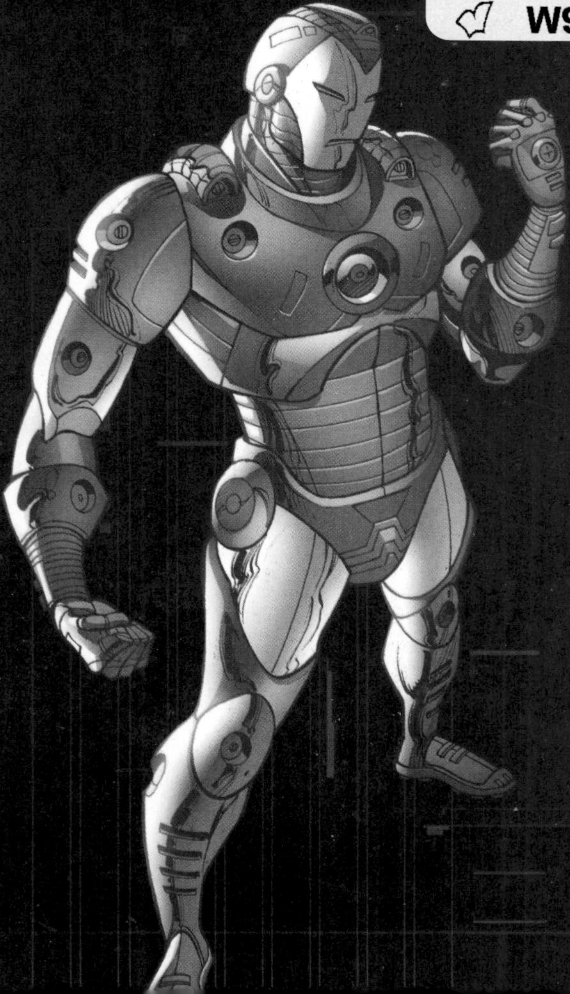

IRON MAN

IRON ARMORY

WRITER: Fred Van Lente
PENCILERS: Rafa Sandoval, James Cordeiro
& Graham Nolan
INKERS: Roger Bonet, Gary Erskine
& Victor Olazaba
COLORISTS: Martegod Gracia & Ulises Arreola
LETTERER: Dave Sharpe

COVER ARTIST: Skottie Young

ASSISTANT EDITOR: Nathan Cosby
EDITOR: Mark Paniccia

COLLECTION EDITOR: Jennifer Grünwald
ASSISTANT EDITORS: Cory Levine & John Denning
EDITOR, SPECIAL PROJECTS: Mark D. Beazley
SENIOR EDITOR, SPECIAL PROJECTS: Jeff Youngquist
SENIOR VICE PRESIDENT OF SALES: David Gabriel
PRODUCTION: Jerry Kalinowski & Jerron Quality Color
VICE PRESIDENT OF CREATIVE: Tom Marvelli

EDITOR IN CHIEF: Joe Quesada
PUBLISHER: Dan Buckley

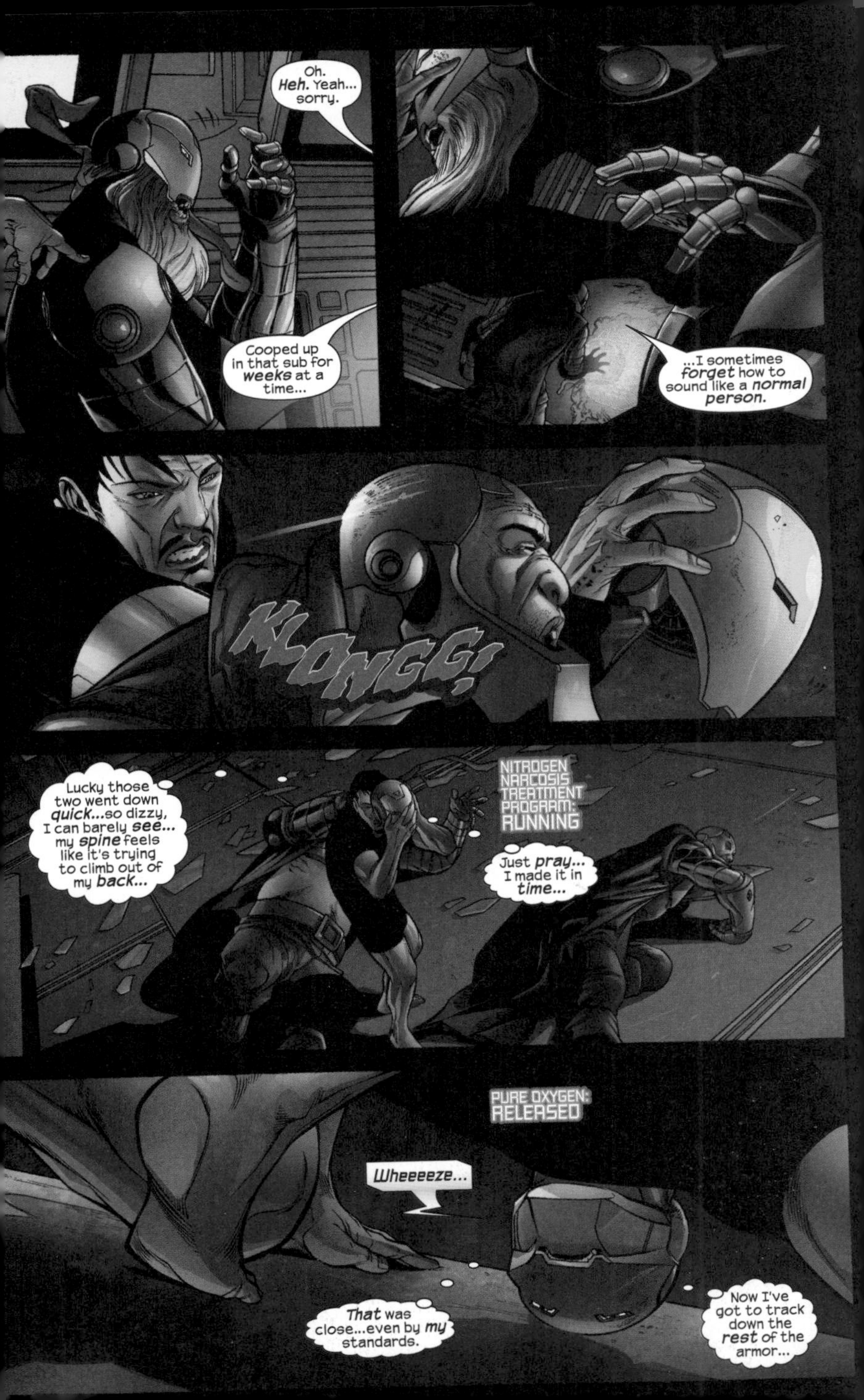

Oh. Heh. Yeah... sorry.
Cooped up in that sub for weeks at a time...
...I sometimes forget how to sound like a normal person.
KLONGG!
Lucky those two went down quick...so dizzy, I can barely see... my spine feels like it's trying to climb out of my back...
NITROGEN NARCOSIS TREATMENT PROGRAM: RUNNING
Just pray... I made it in time...
PURE OXYGEN: RELEASED
Wheeeeze...
That was close...even by my standards.
Now I've got to track down the rest of the armor...

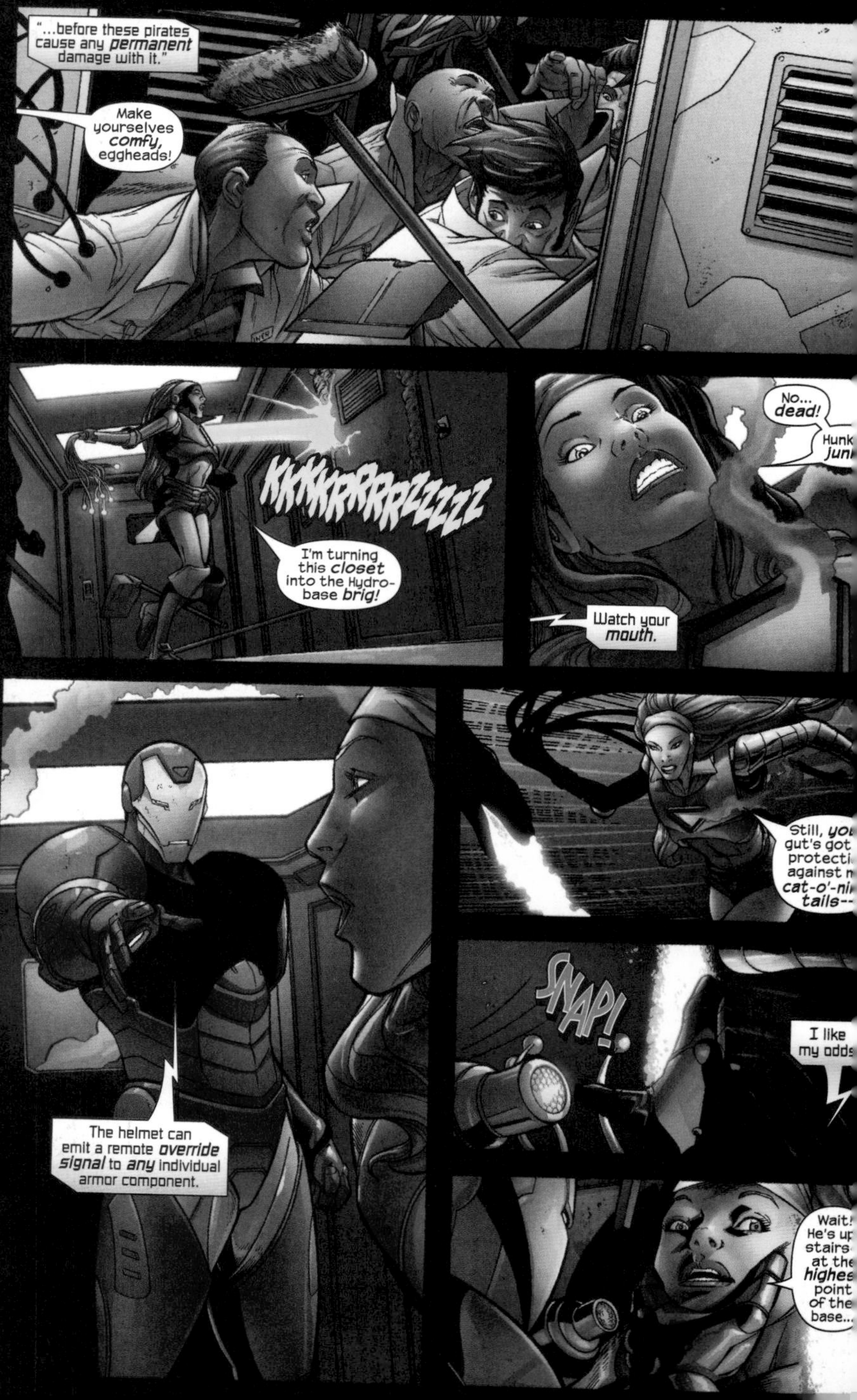
"...before these pirates cause any permanent damage with it."
Make yourselves comfy, eggheads!
KKKKRRRRRZZZZZ
I'm turning this closet into the Hydro-base brig!
No... dead!
Hunk
Watch your mouth.
The helmet can emit a remote override signal to any individual armor component.
Still,
gut's got
protecti
against
cat-o'-ni
tails--
SNAP!
I like my odds
Wait!
He's up
stairs
at the
highes
point
of the
base...

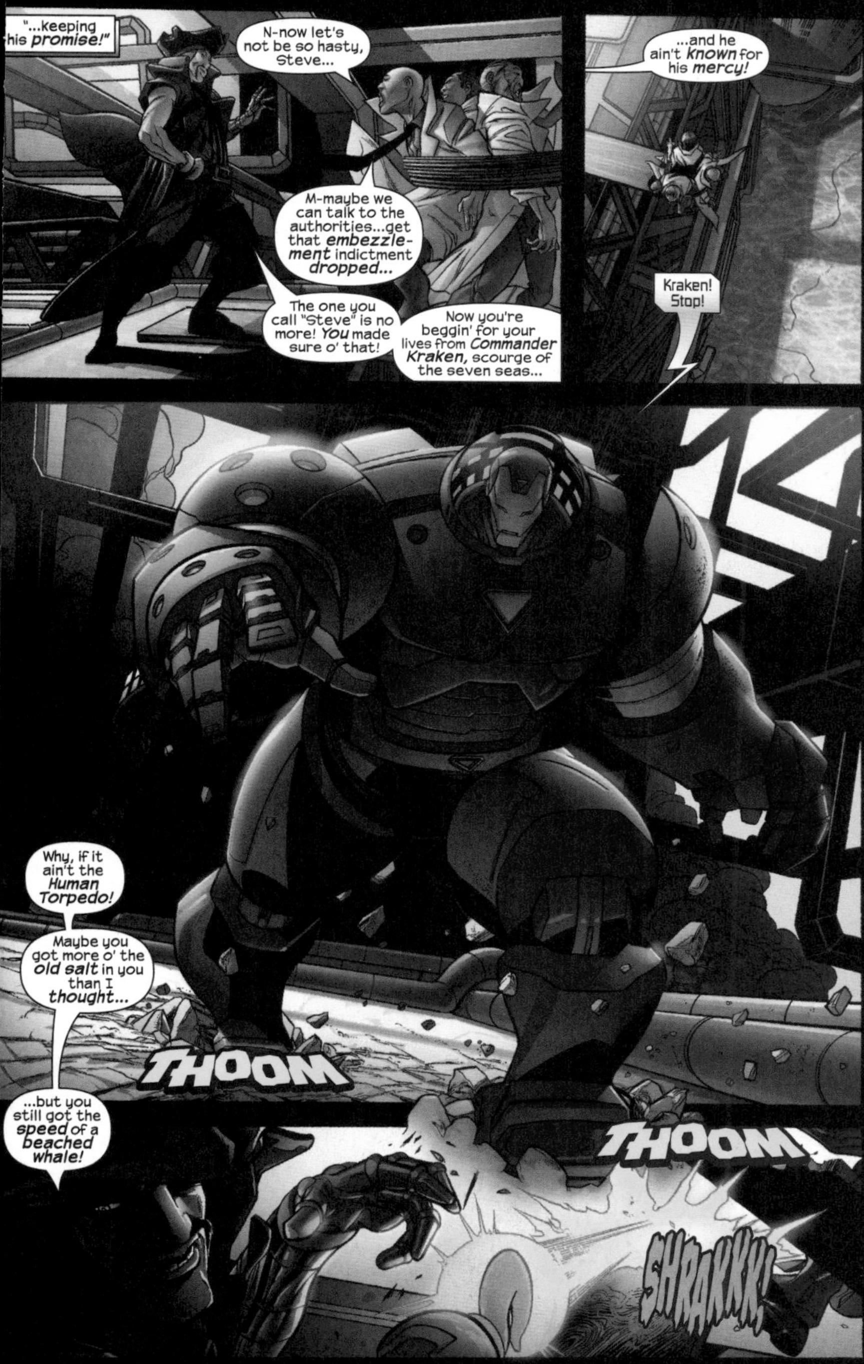
"...keeping his promise!"
N-now let's not be so hasty, Steve...
M-maybe we can talk to the authorities...get that embezzlement indictment dropped...
The one you call "Steve" is no more! You made sure o' that!
Now you're beggin' for your lives from Commander Kraken, scourge of the seven seas...
...and he ain't known for his mercy!
Kraken! Stop!
Why, if it ain't the Human Torpedo!
Maybe you got more o' the old salt in you than I thought...
THOOM
...but you still got the speed of a beached whale!
THOOM!
SHRAKK!

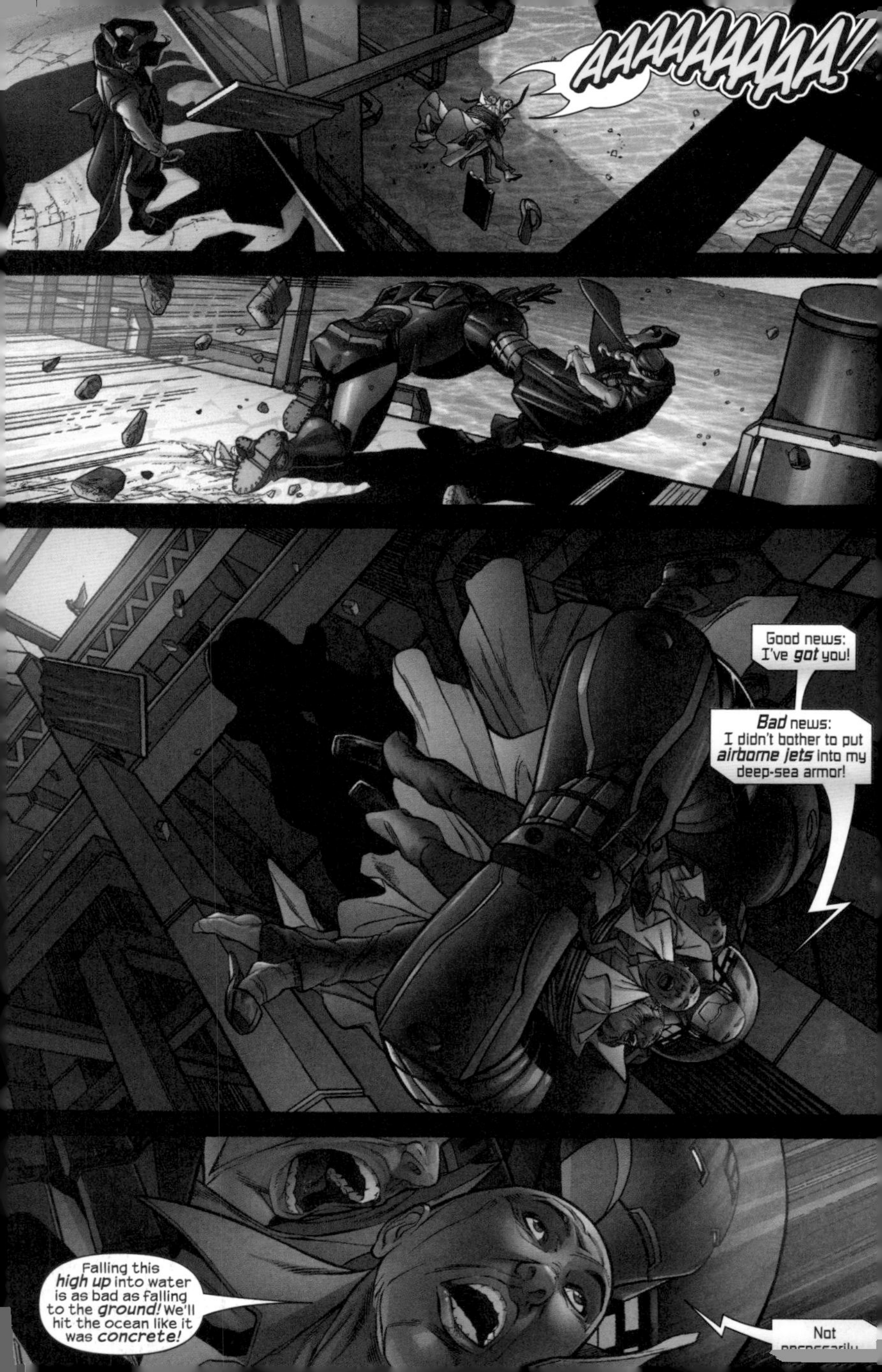
AAAAAAAAA!
Good news: I've *got* you!
Bad news: I didn't bother to put *airborne jets* into my deep-sea armor!
Falling this *high up* into water is as bad as falling to the *ground!* We'll hit the ocean like it was *concrete!*
Not

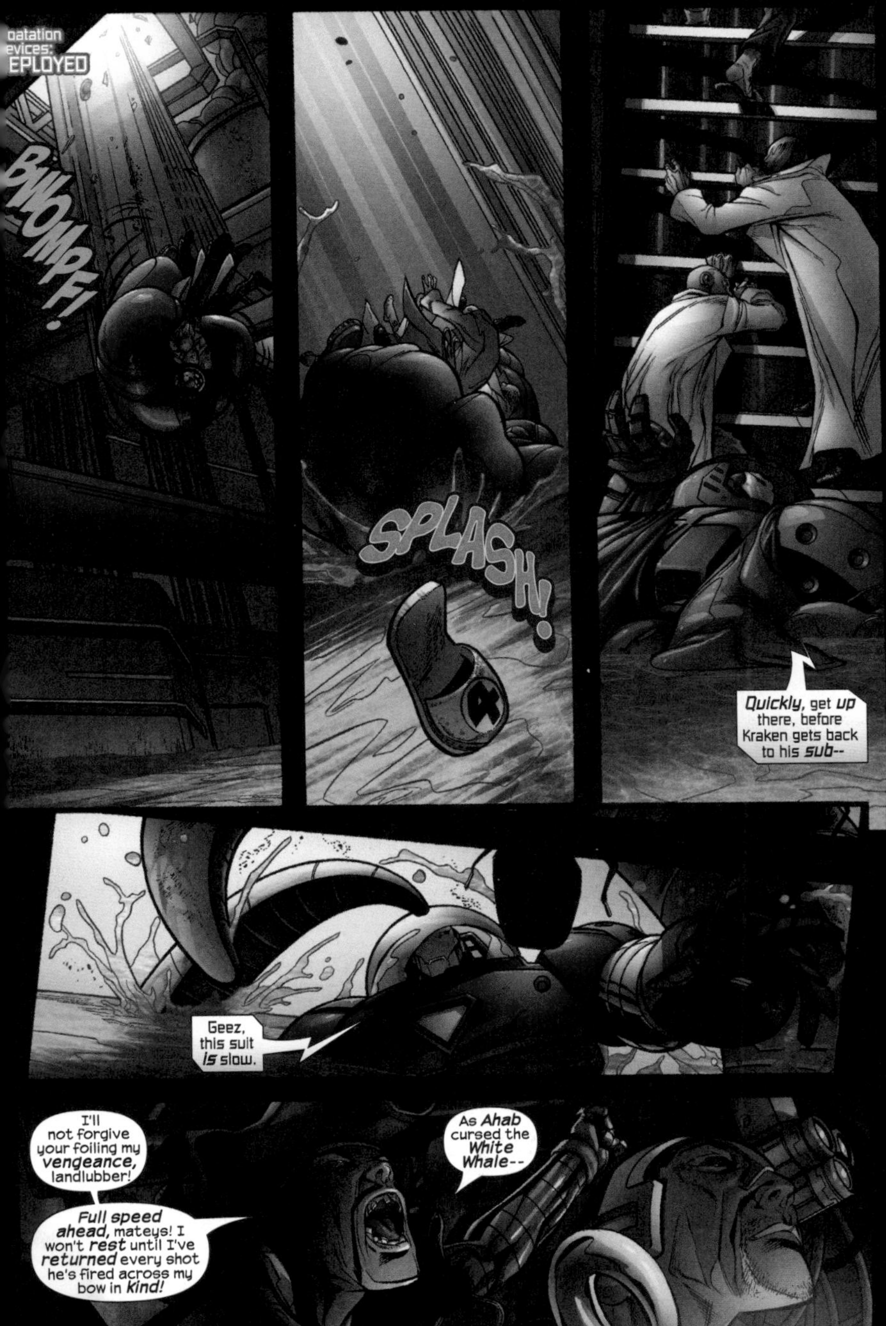

oatation evices: EPLOYED
BWOMPF!
SPLASH!
Quickly, get up there, before Kraken gets back to his sub--
Geez, this suit is slow.
I'll not forgive your foiling my vengeance, landlubber!
Full speed ahead, mateys! I won't rest until I've returned every shot he's fired across my bow in kind!
As Ahab cursed the White Whale--

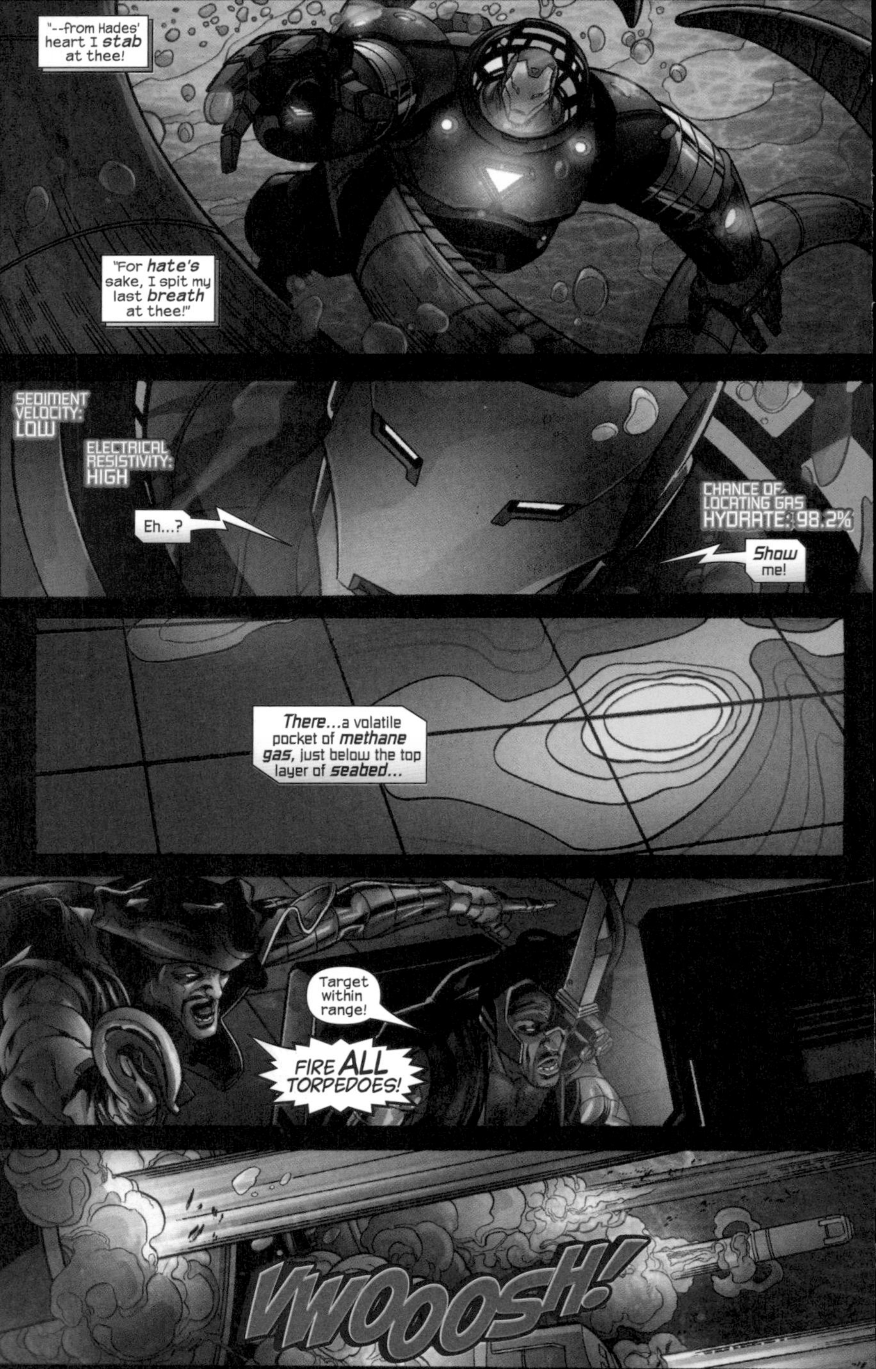

"--from Hades' heart I stab at thee!
"For hate's sake, I spit my last breath at thee!"
SEDIMENT VELOCITY: LOW
ELECTRICAL RESISTIVITY: HIGH
Eh...?
CHANCE OF LOCATING GAS HYDRATE: 98.2%
Show me!
There...a volatile pocket of methane gas, just below the top layer of seabed...
Target within range!
FIRE ALL TORPEDOES!
VWOOOOSH!

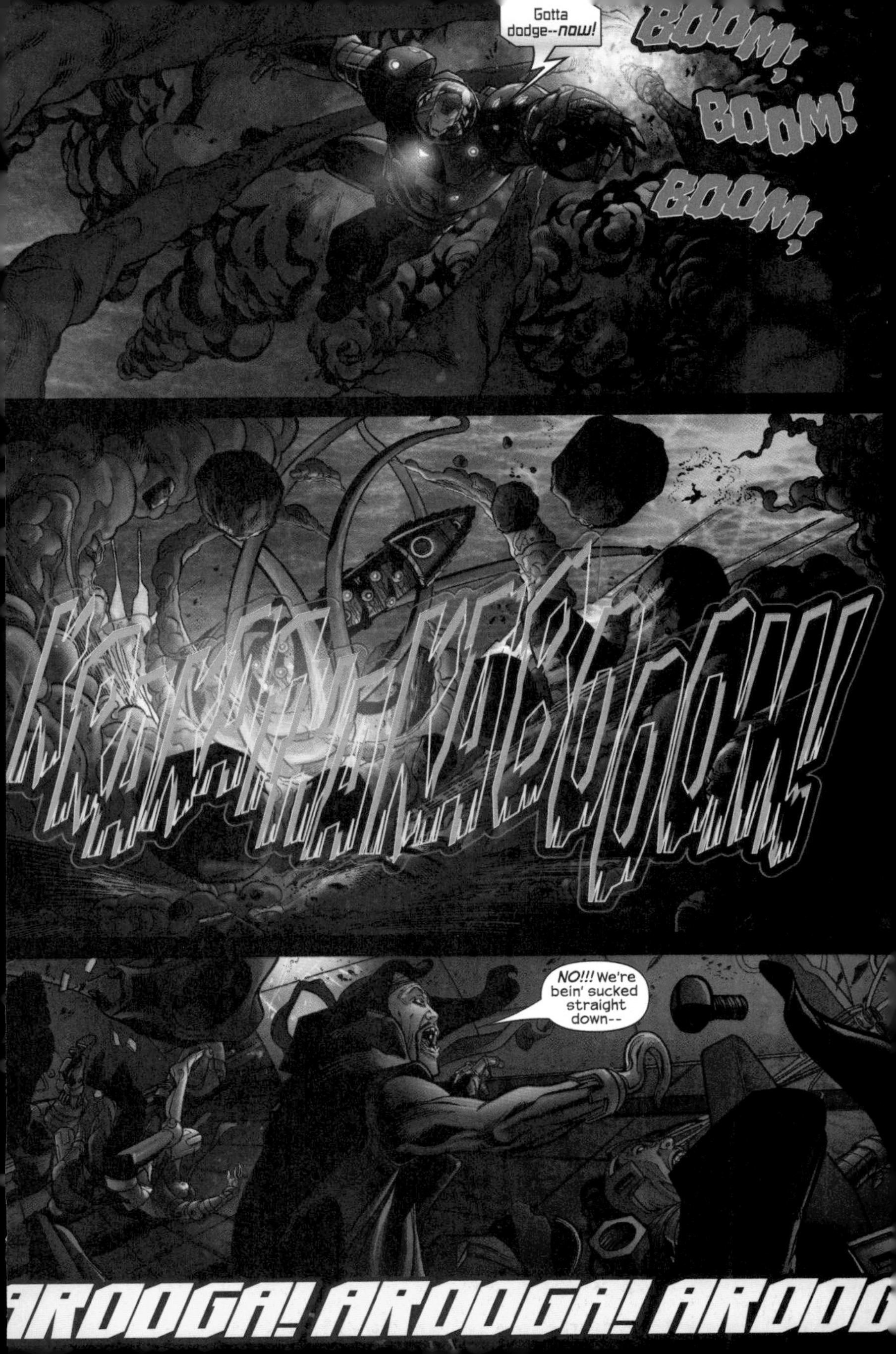
Gotta dodge--*now!*
BOOM!
BOOM!
BOOM!
NO!!! We're bein' sucked straight down--
ROOGA! AROOGA! AROOG

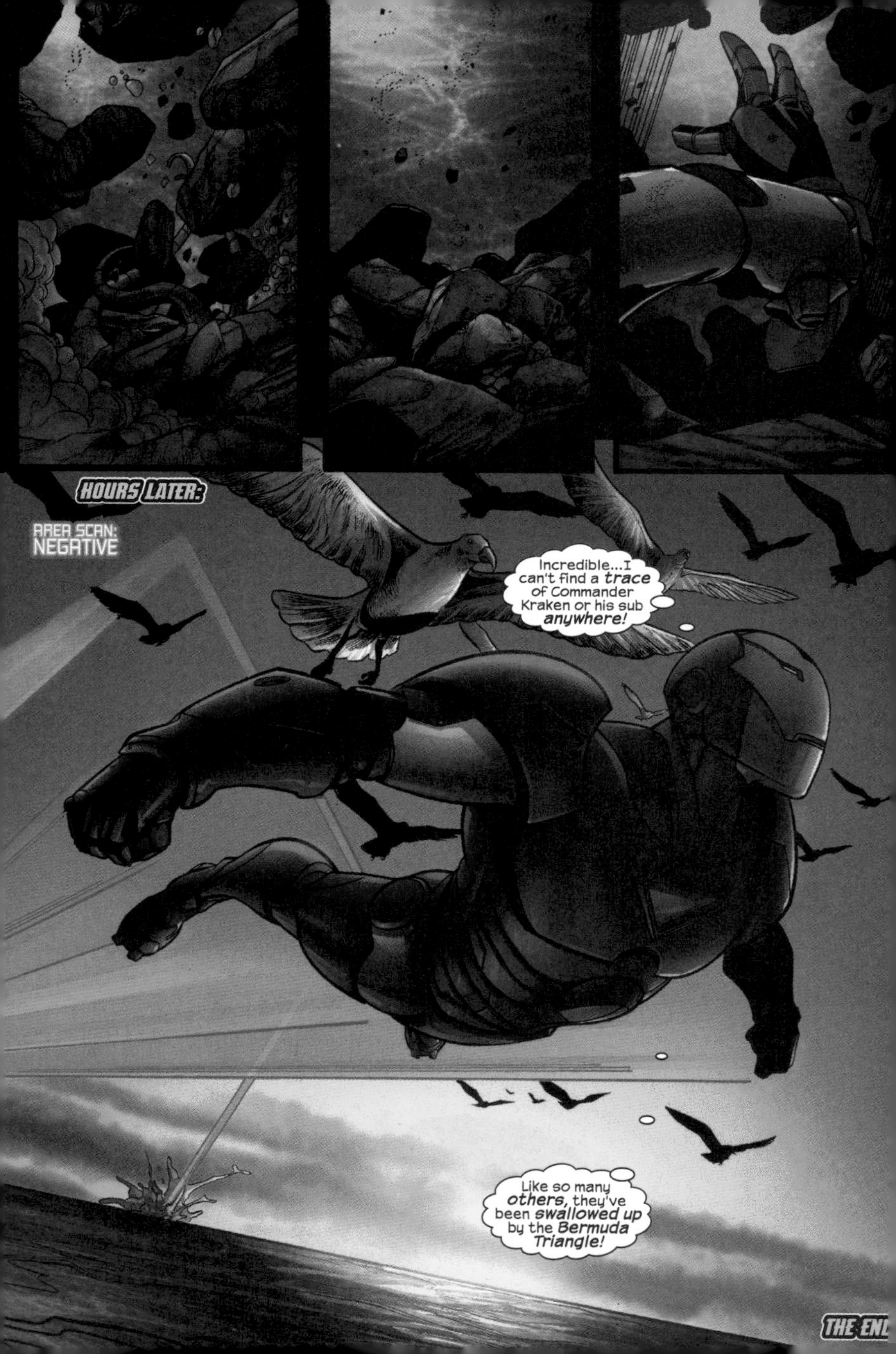
HOURS LATER:
AREA SCAN: NEGATIVE
Incredible...I can't find a trace of Commander Kraken or his sub anywhere!
Like so many others, they've been swallowed up by the Bermuda Triangle!
THE END

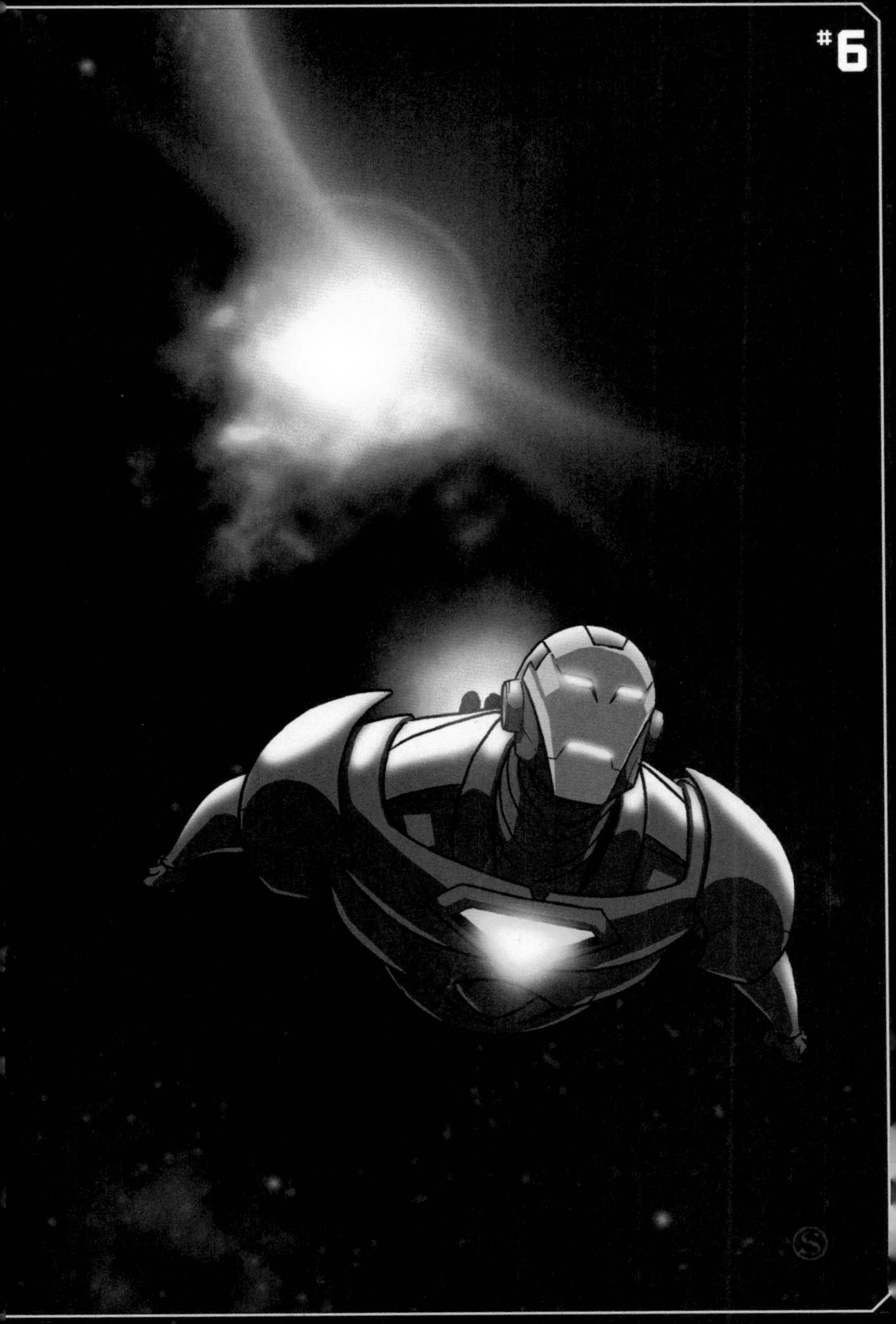
#6

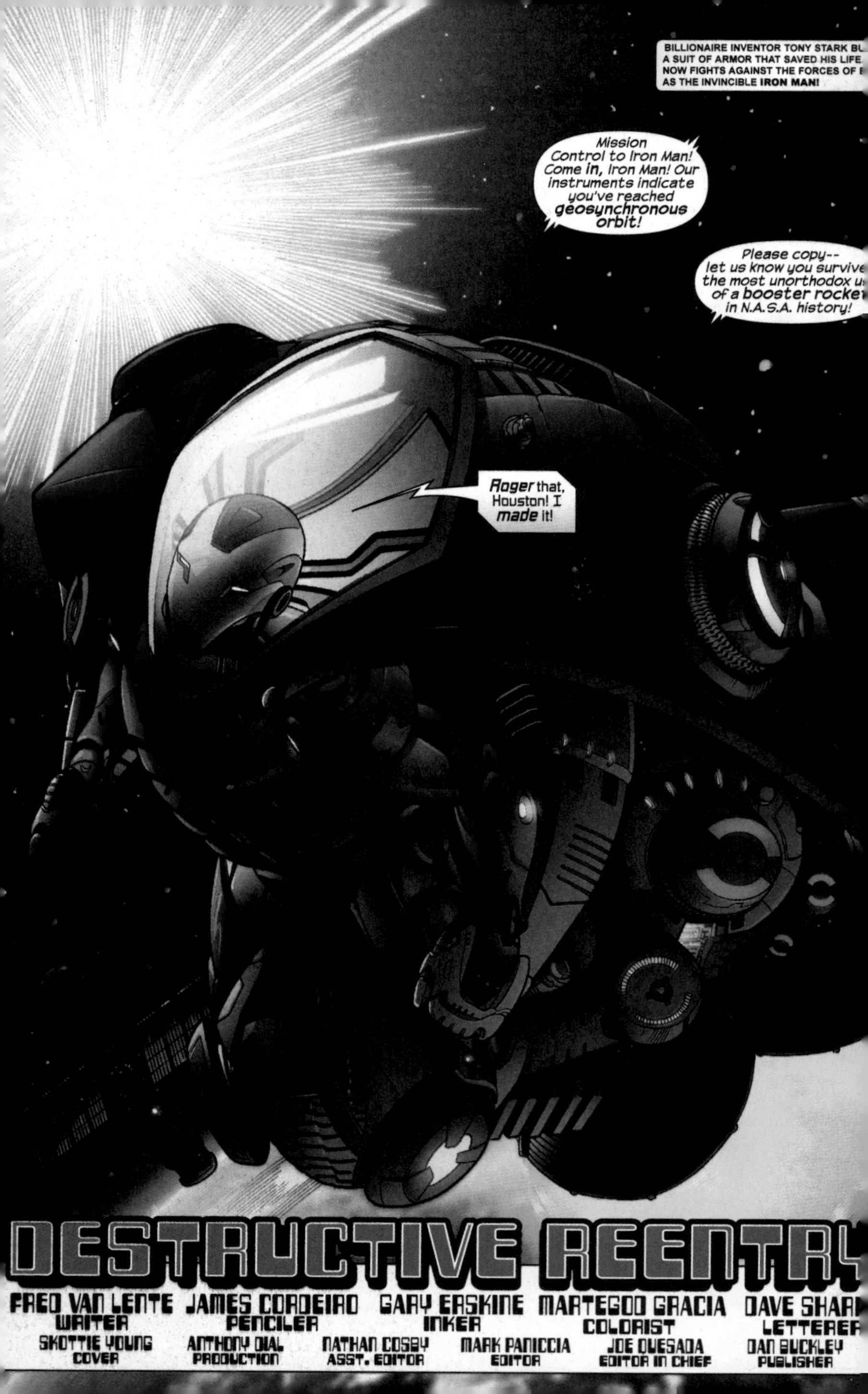

BILLIONAIRE INVENTOR TONY STARK BU
A SUIT OF ARMOR THAT SAVED HIS LIFE.
NOW FIGHTS AGAINST THE FORCES OF
AS THE INVINCIBLE IRON MAN!
Mission Control to Iron Man! Come in, Iron Man! Our instruments indicate you've reached geosynchronous orbit!
Please copy-- let us know you survive the most unorthodox u of a booster rocke in N.A.S.A. history!
Roger that, Houston! I made it!
DESTRUCTIVE REENTR
FRED VAN LENTE WRITER
JAMES CORDEIRO PENCILER
GARY ERSKINE INKER
MARTEGOD GRACIA COLORIST
DAVE SHAR LETTERER
SKOTTIE YOUNG COVER
ANTHONY DIAL PRODUCTION
NATHAN COSBY ASST. EDITOR
MARK PANICCIA EDITOR
JOE QUESADA EDITOR IN CHIEF
DAN BUCKLEY PUBLISHER

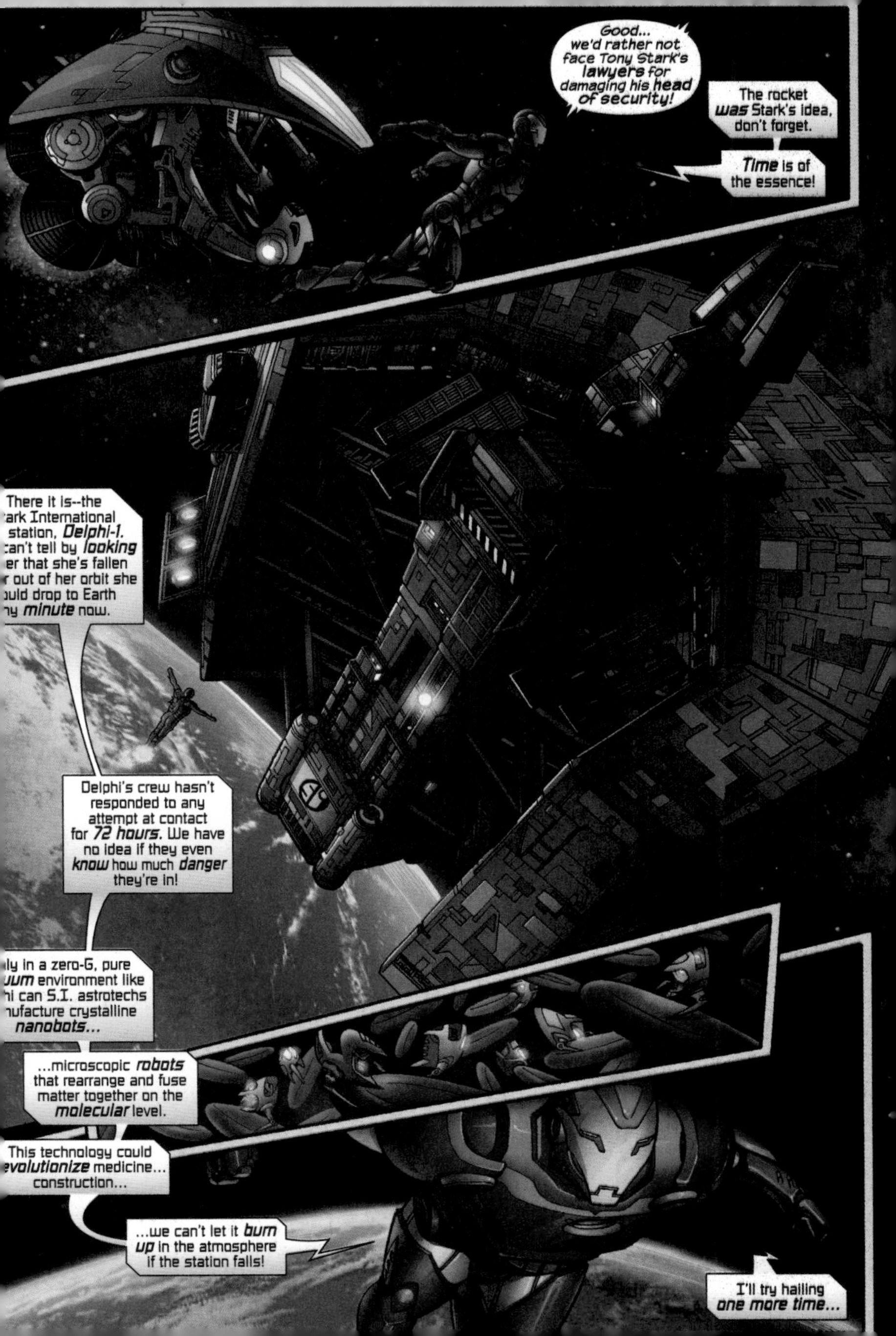
Good... we'd rather not face Tony Stark's lawyers for damaging his head of security!
The rocket was Stark's idea, don't forget.
Time is of the essence!
There it is--the ark International station, Delphi-1. an't tell by looking er that she's fallen out of her orbit she uld drop to Earth y minute now.
Delphi's crew hasn't responded to any attempt at contact for 72 hours. We have no idea if they even know how much danger they're in!
ly in a zero-G, pure uum environment like i can S.I. astrotechs ufacture crystalline nanobots...
...microscopic robots that rearrange and fuse matter together on the molecular level.
This technology could evolutionize medicine... construction...
...we can't let it burn up in the atmosphere if the station falls!
I'll try hailing one more time...

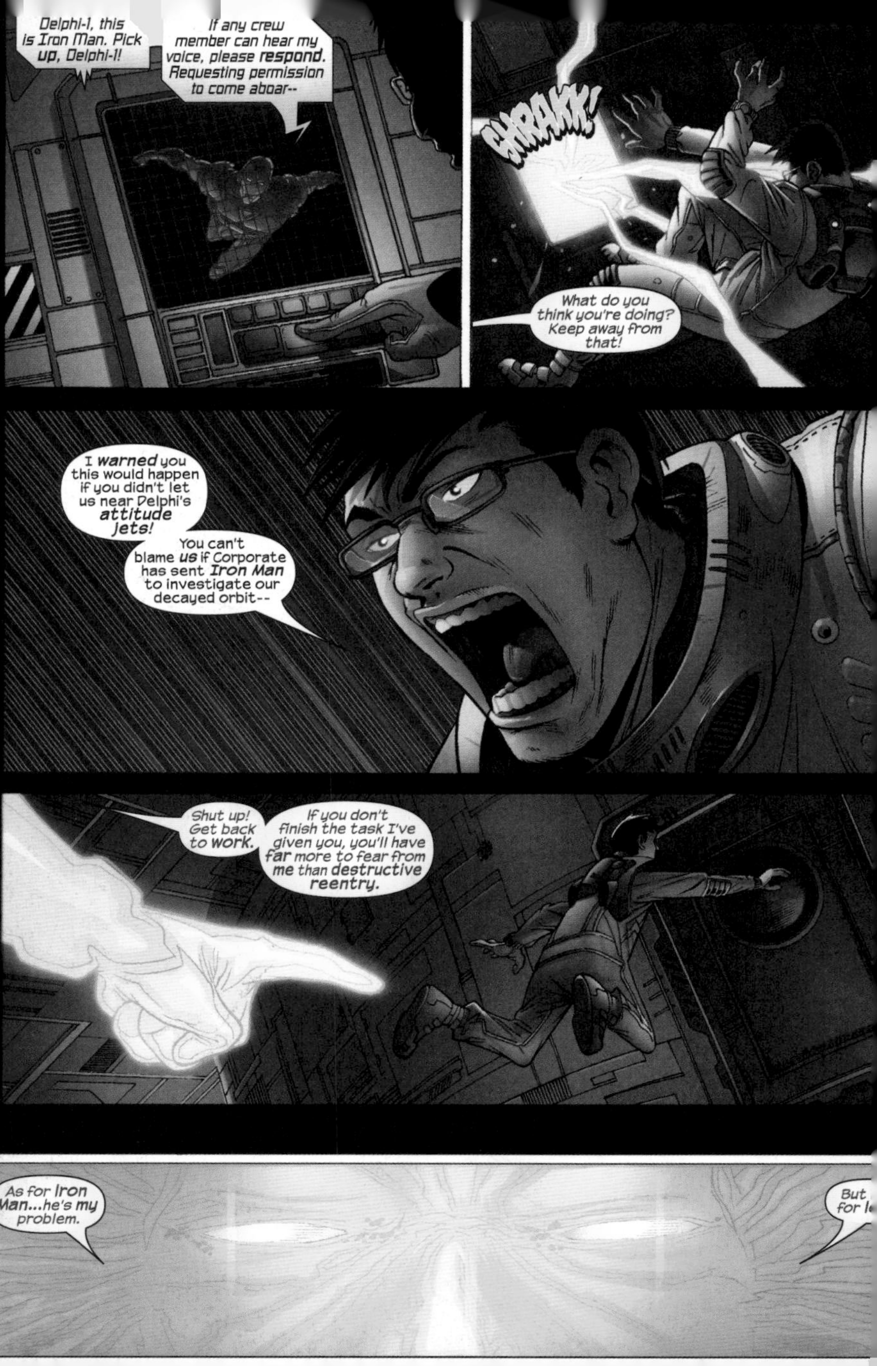
Delphi-1, this is Iron Man. Pick up, Delphi-1!
If any crew member can hear my voice, please respond. Requesting permission to come aboar--
SHRAKK!
What do you think you're doing? Keep away from that!
I warned you this would happen if you didn't let us near Delphi's attitude jets!
You can't blame us if Corporate has sent Iron Man to investigate our decayed orbit--
Shut up! Get back to work.
If you don't finish the task I've given you, you'll have far more to fear from me than destructive reentry.
As for Iron Man...he's my problem.

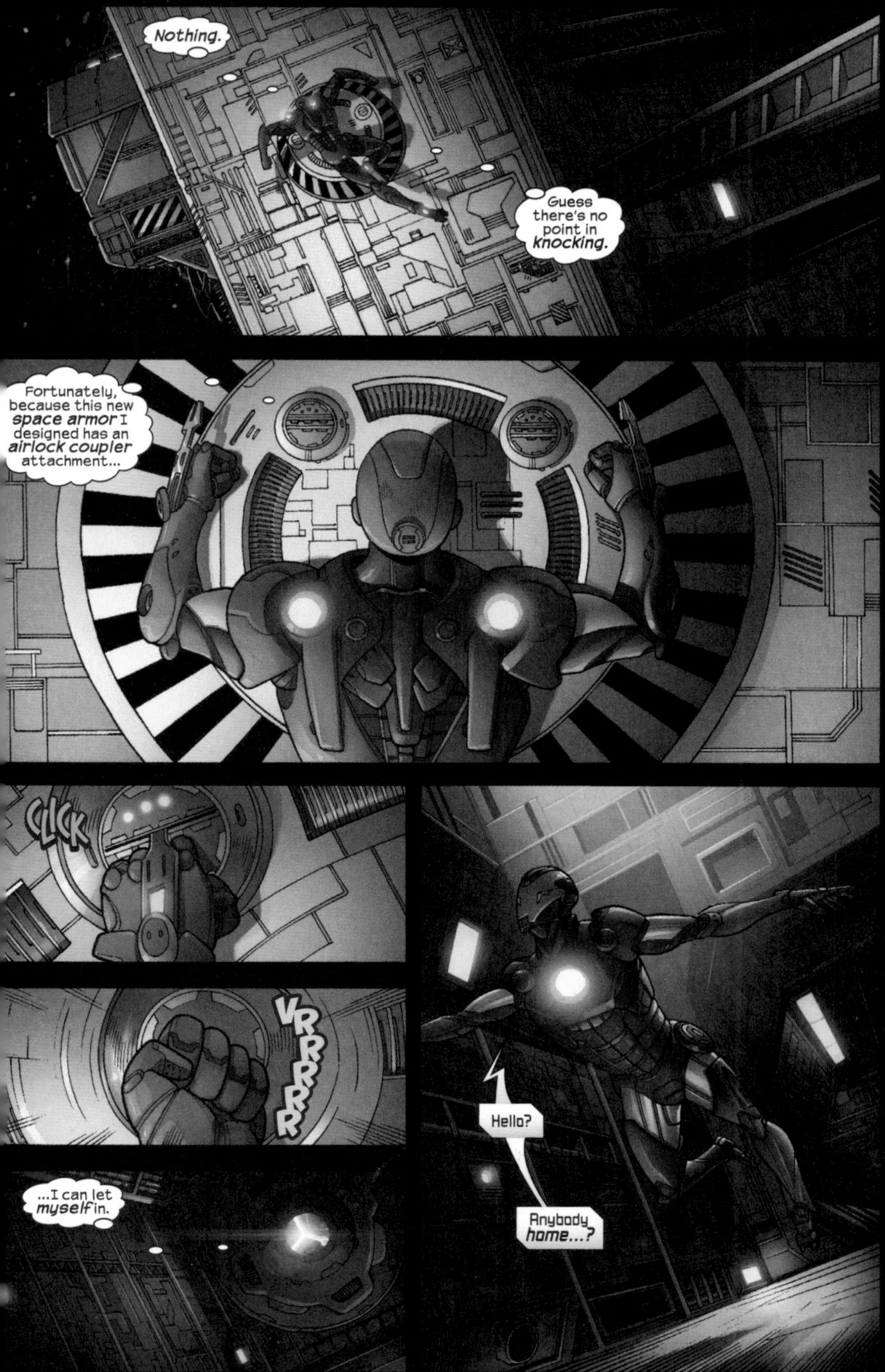
Nothing.
Guess there's no point in knocking.
Fortunately, because this new space armor I designed has an airlock coupler attachment...
CLICK
VRRRRR
...I can let myself in.
Hello?
Anybody home...?

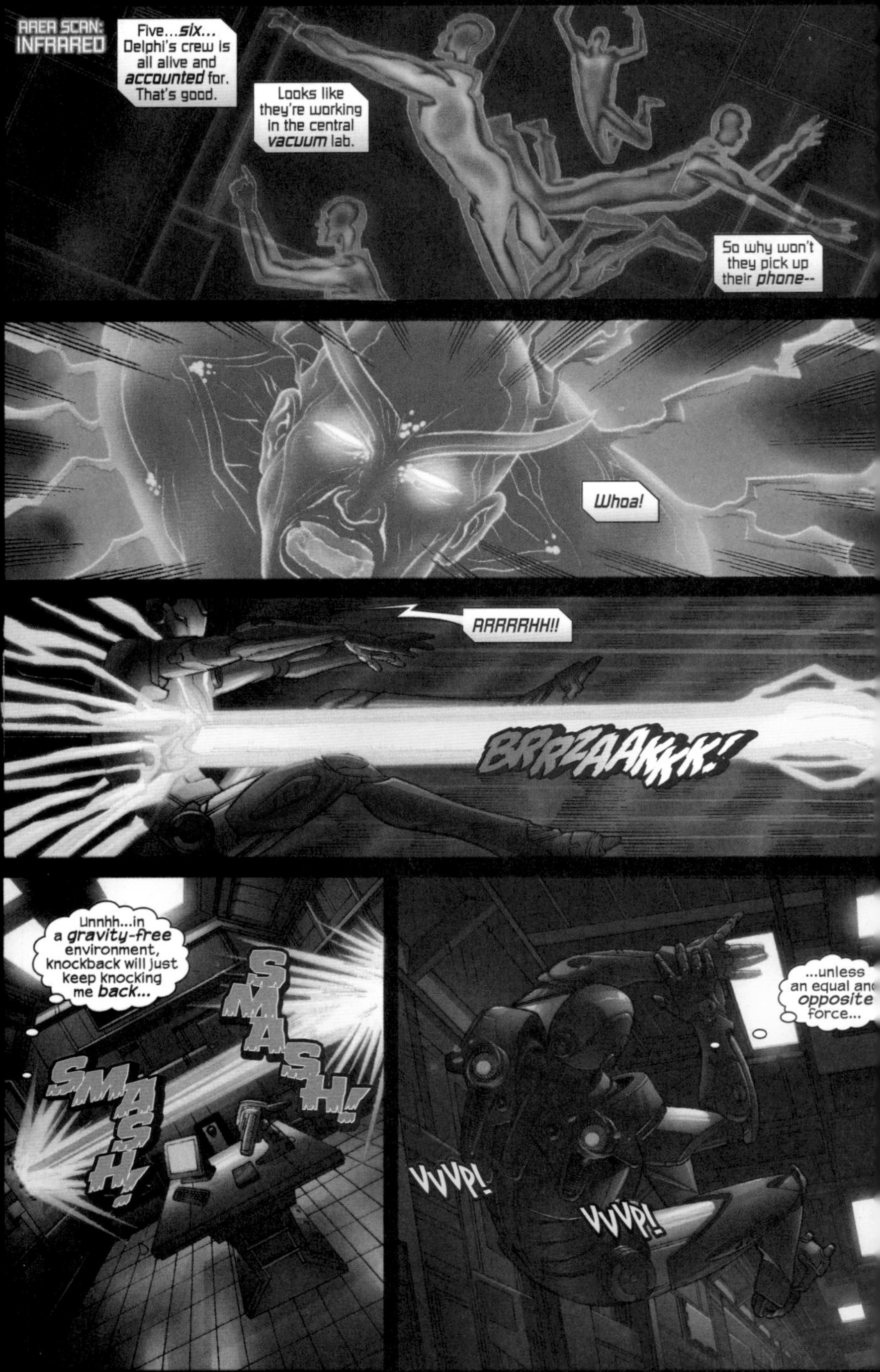
AREA SCAN: INFRARED
Five...six... Delphi's crew is all alive and accounted for. That's good.
Looks like they're working in the central vacuum lab.
So why won't they pick up their phone--
Whoa!
AAAAAHH!!
BRRZAAKKK!
Unnhh...in a gravity-free environment, knockback will just keep knocking me back...
SMASH!
SMASH!
...unless an equal and opposite force...
VVVP!
VVVP!

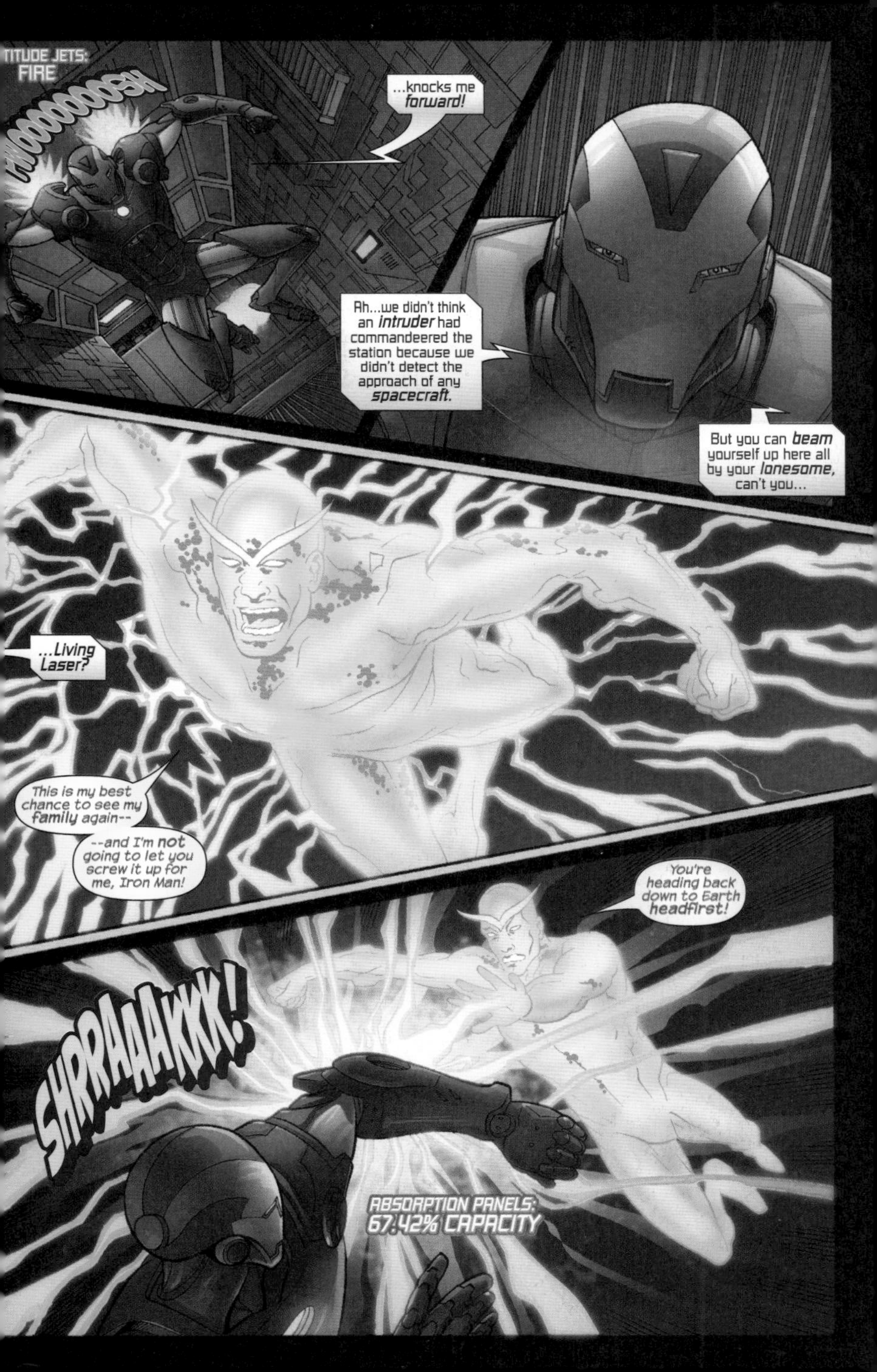

TITUDE JETS:
FIRE
WHOOOOOOOSH
...knocks me forward!
Ah...we didn't think an intruder had commandeered the station because we didn't detect the approach of any spacecraft.
But you can beam yourself up here all by your lonesome, can't you...
...Living Laser?
This is my best chance to see my family again--
--and I'm not going to let you screw it up for me, Iron Man!
You're heading back down to Earth headfirst!
SHRAAAKKK!
ABSORPTION PANELS:
67.42% CAPACITY

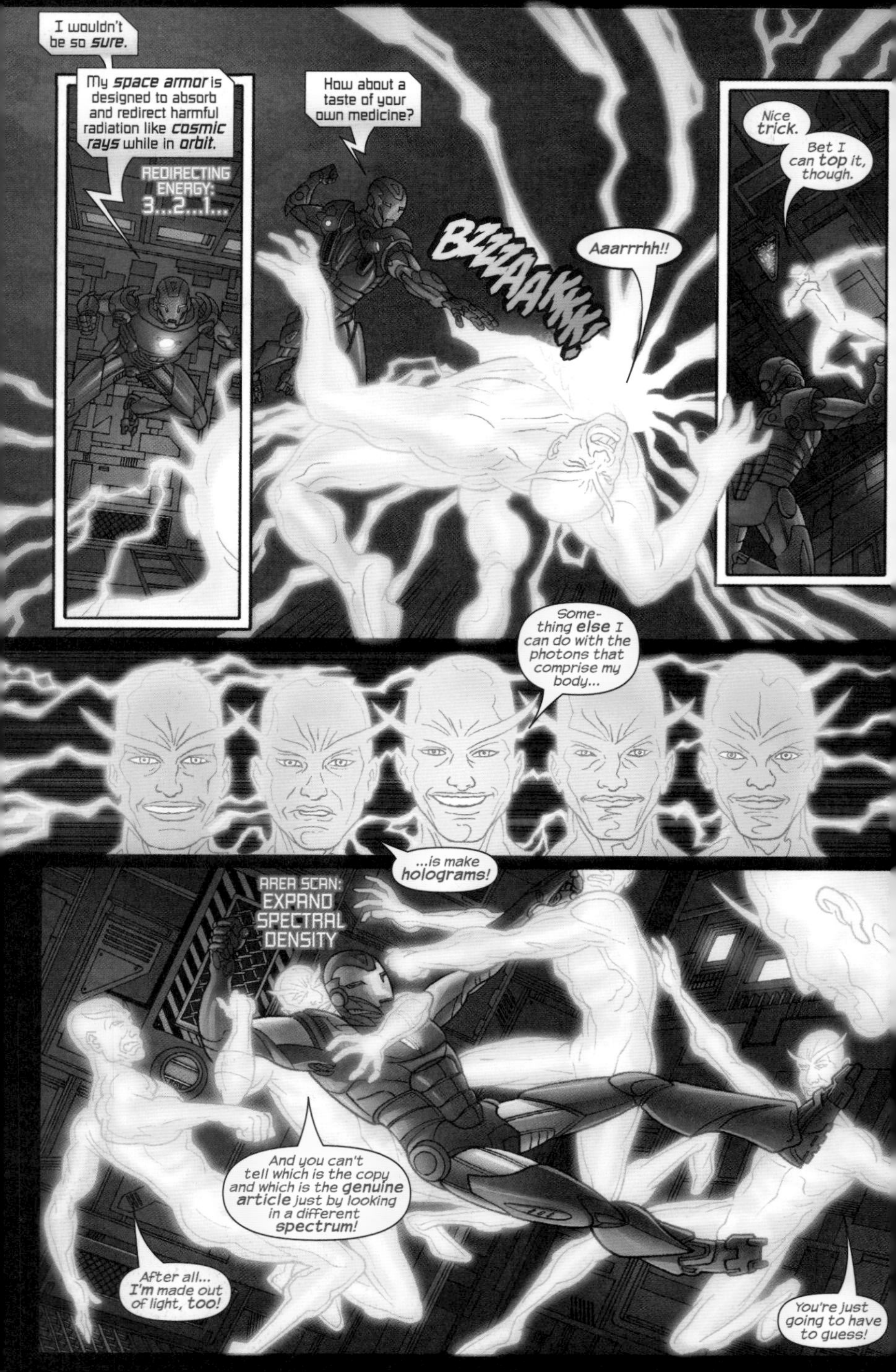
I wouldn't be so sure.
My space armor is designed to absorb and redirect harmful radiation like cosmic rays while in orbit.
REDIRECTING ENERGY: 3...2...1...
How about a taste of your own medicine?
BZZAAKKK!
Aaarrrhh!!
Nice trick.
Bet I can top it, though.
Some-thing else I can do with the photons that comprise my body...
...is make holograms!
AREA SCAN: EXPAND SPECTRAL DENSITY
And you can't tell which is the copy and which is the genuine article just by looking in a different spectrum!
After all... I'm made out of light, too!
You're just going to have to guess!

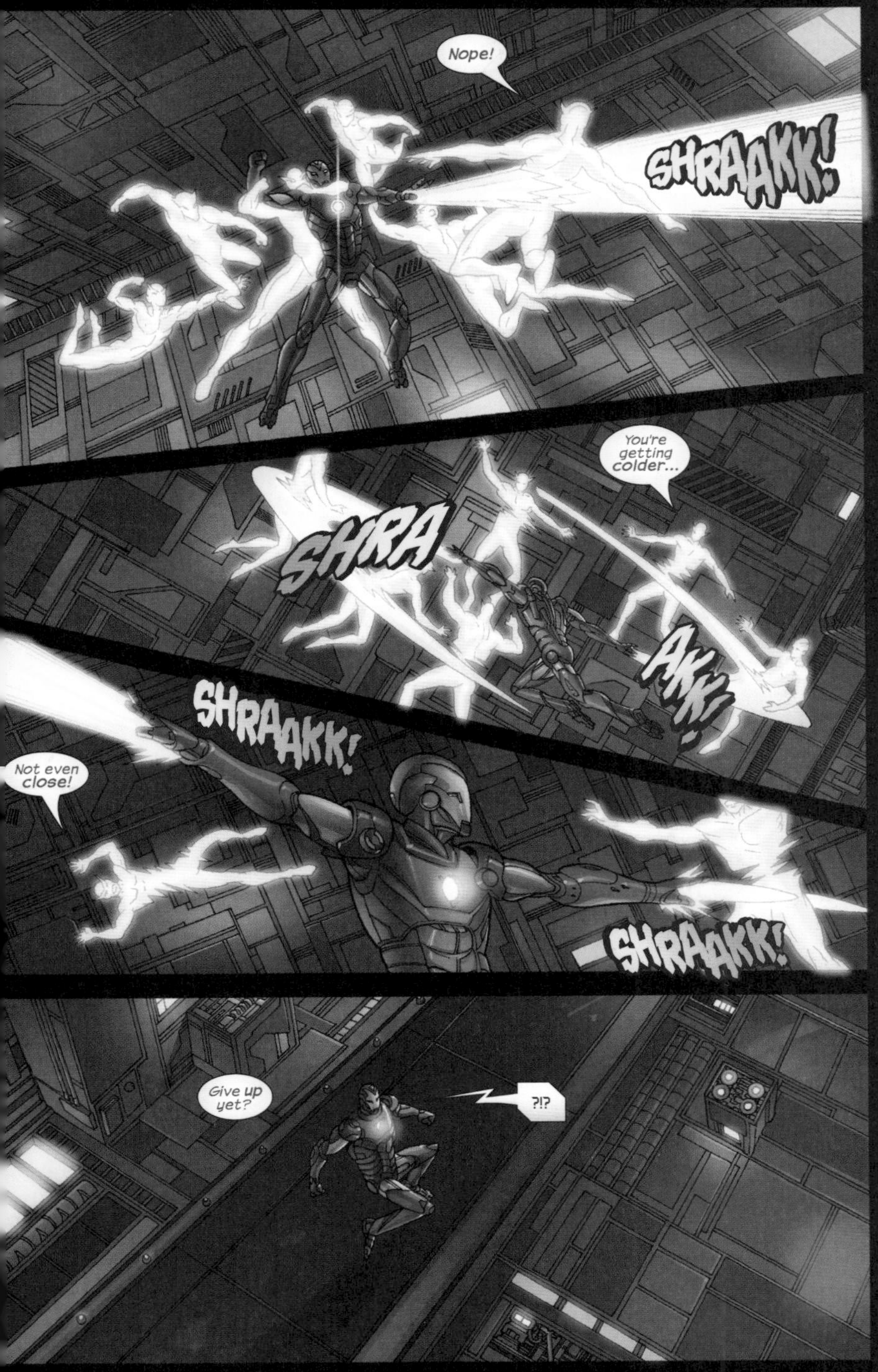
Nope!
SHRAAKK!
You're getting colder...
SHRA
AKK!
SHRAAKK!
Not even close!
SHRAAKK!
Give up yet?
?!?

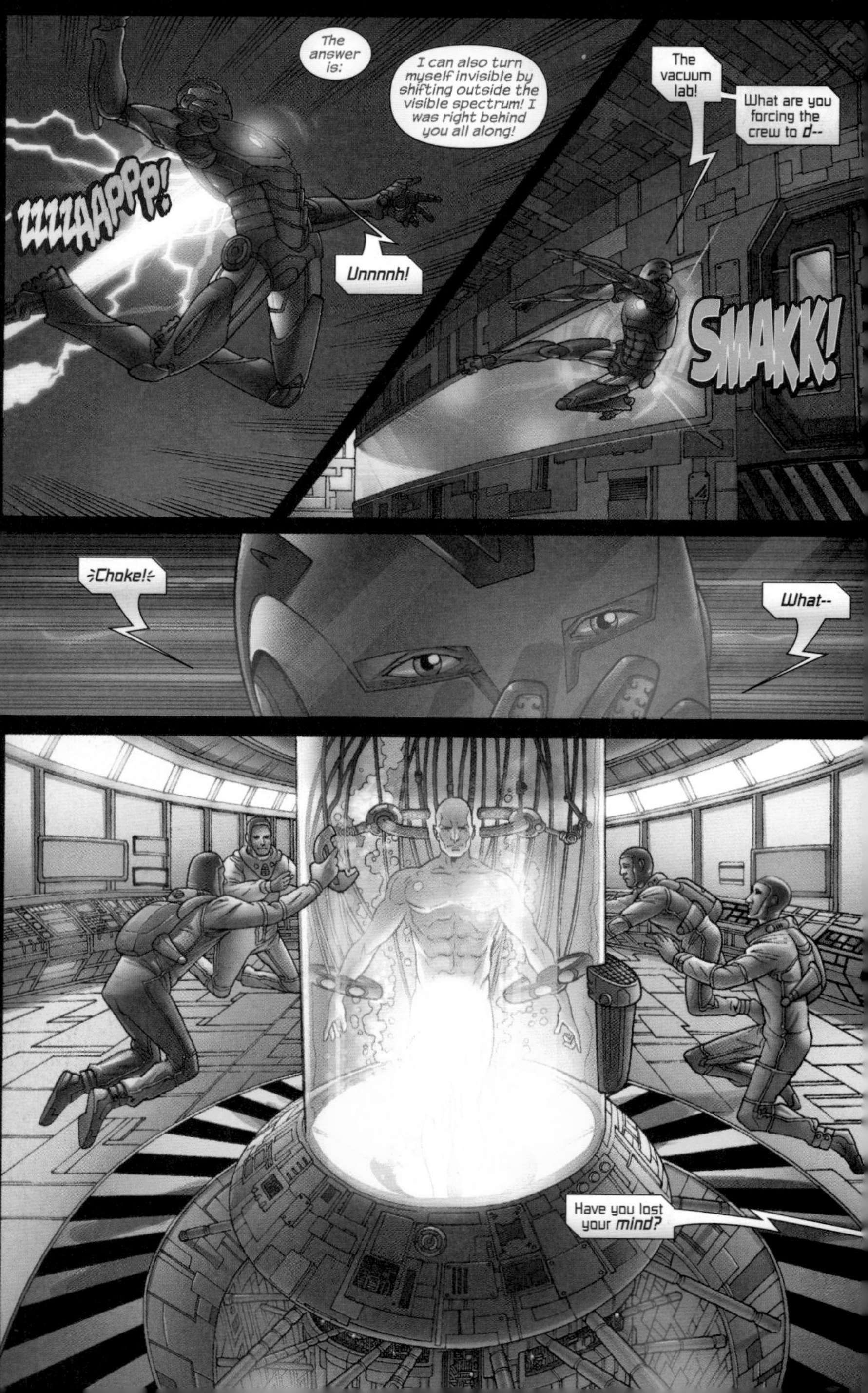

The answer is:
I can also turn myself invisible by shifting outside the visible spectrum! I was right behind you all along!
ZZZZAPPP!
Unnnnh!
The vacuum lab!
What are you forcing the crew to d--
SMAKK!
Choke!
What--
Have you lost your mind?

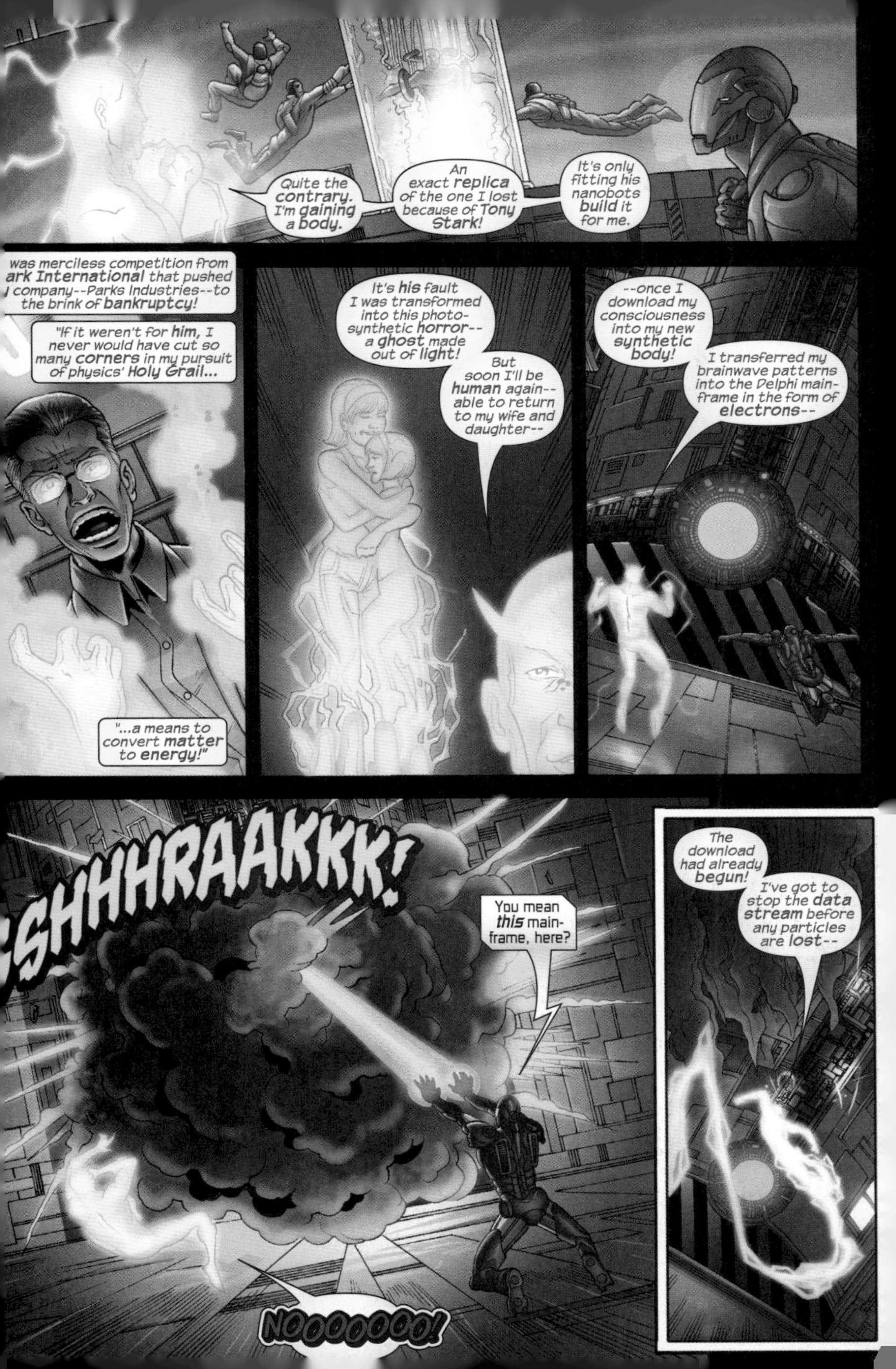
Quite the contrary. I'm gaining a body.
An exact replica of the one I lost because of Tony Stark!
It's only fitting his nanobots build it for me.
was merciless competition from ark International that pushed company--Parks Industries--to the brink of bankruptcy!
"If it weren't for him, I never would have cut so many corners in my pursuit of physics' Holy Grail...
"...a means to convert matter to energy!"
It's his fault I was transformed into this photo-synthetic horror--a ghost made out of light!
But soon I'll be human again--able to return to my wife and daughter--
--once I download my consciousness into my new synthetic body!
I transferred my brainwave patterns into the Delphi main-frame in the form of electrons--
SHHHRAAKKK!
You mean this main-frame, here?
NOOOOOOO!
The download had already begun!
I've got to stop the data stream before any particles are lost--

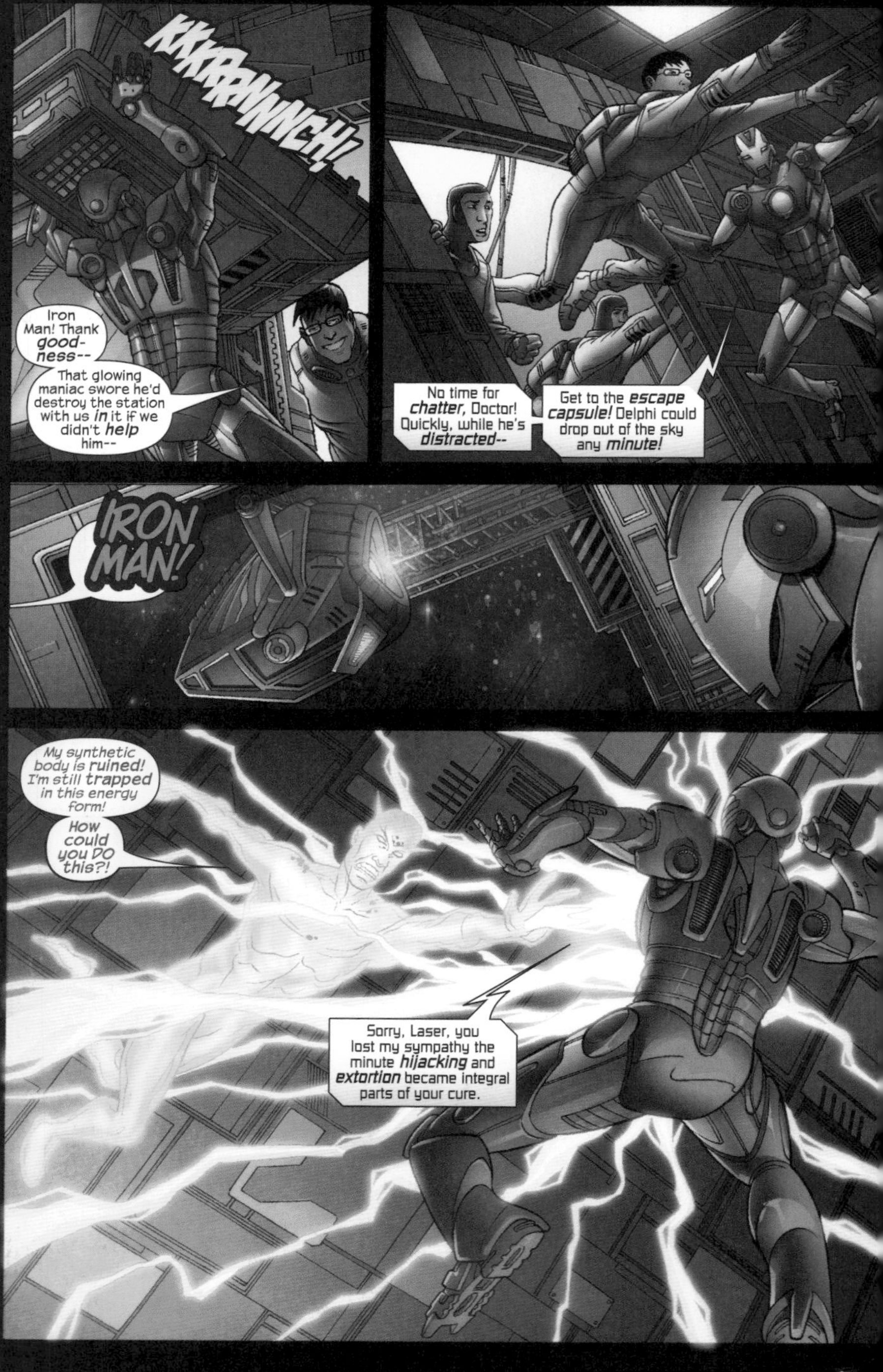

KKKRRNNNCH!!
Iron Man! Thank goodness--
That glowing maniac swore he'd destroy the station with us in it if we didn't help him--
No time for chatter, Doctor! Quickly, while he's distracted--
Get to the escape capsule! Delphi could drop out of the sky any minute!
IRON MAN!
My synthetic body is ruined! I'm still trapped in this energy form!
How could you DO this?!
Sorry, Laser, you lost my sympathy the minute hijacking and extortion became integral parts of your cure.

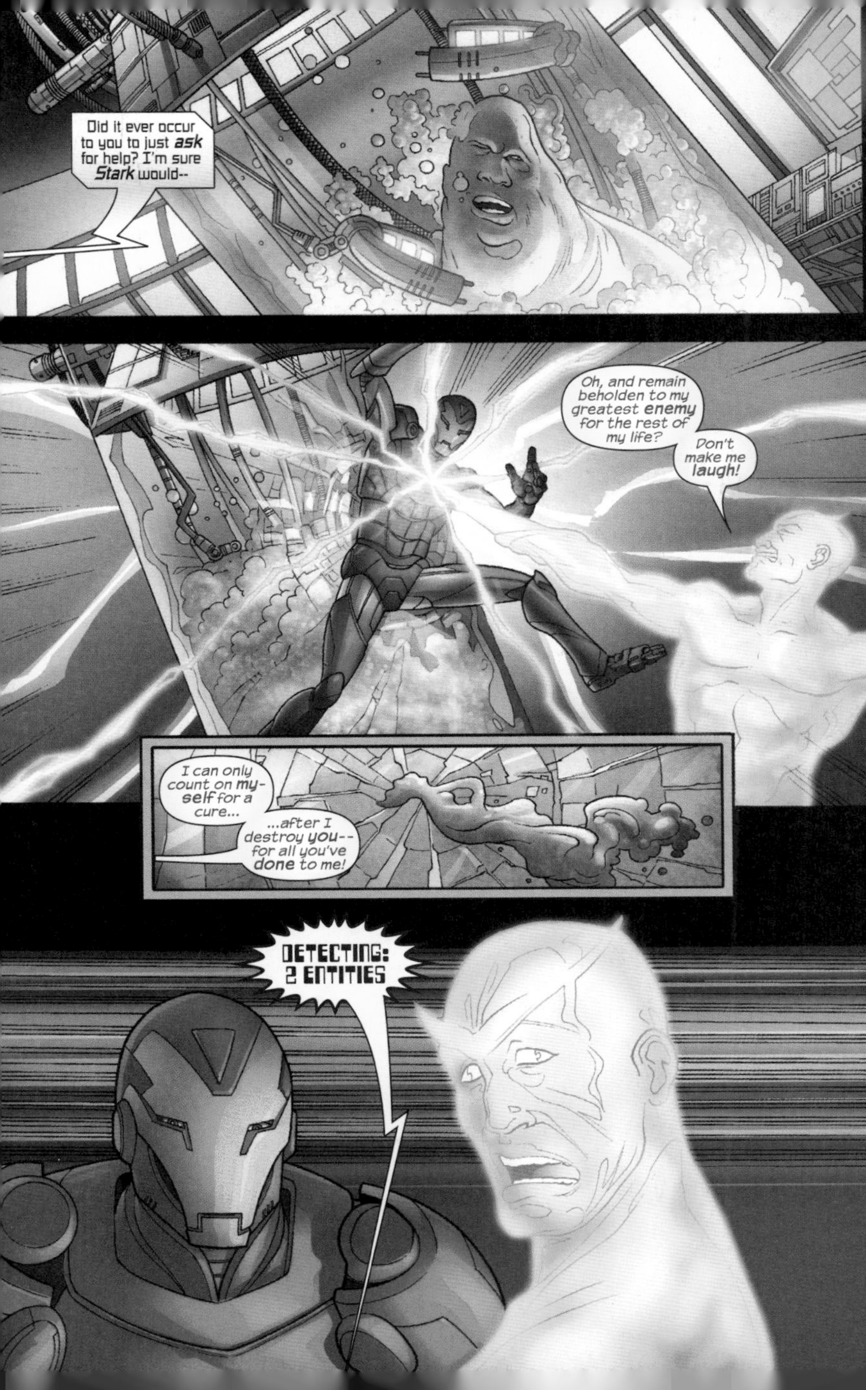

Did it ever occur to you to just ask for help? I'm sure Stark would--
Oh, and remain beholden to my greatest enemy for the rest of my life?
Don't make me laugh!
I can only count on myself for a cure...
...after I destroy you--for all you've done to me!
DETECTING: 2 ENTITIES

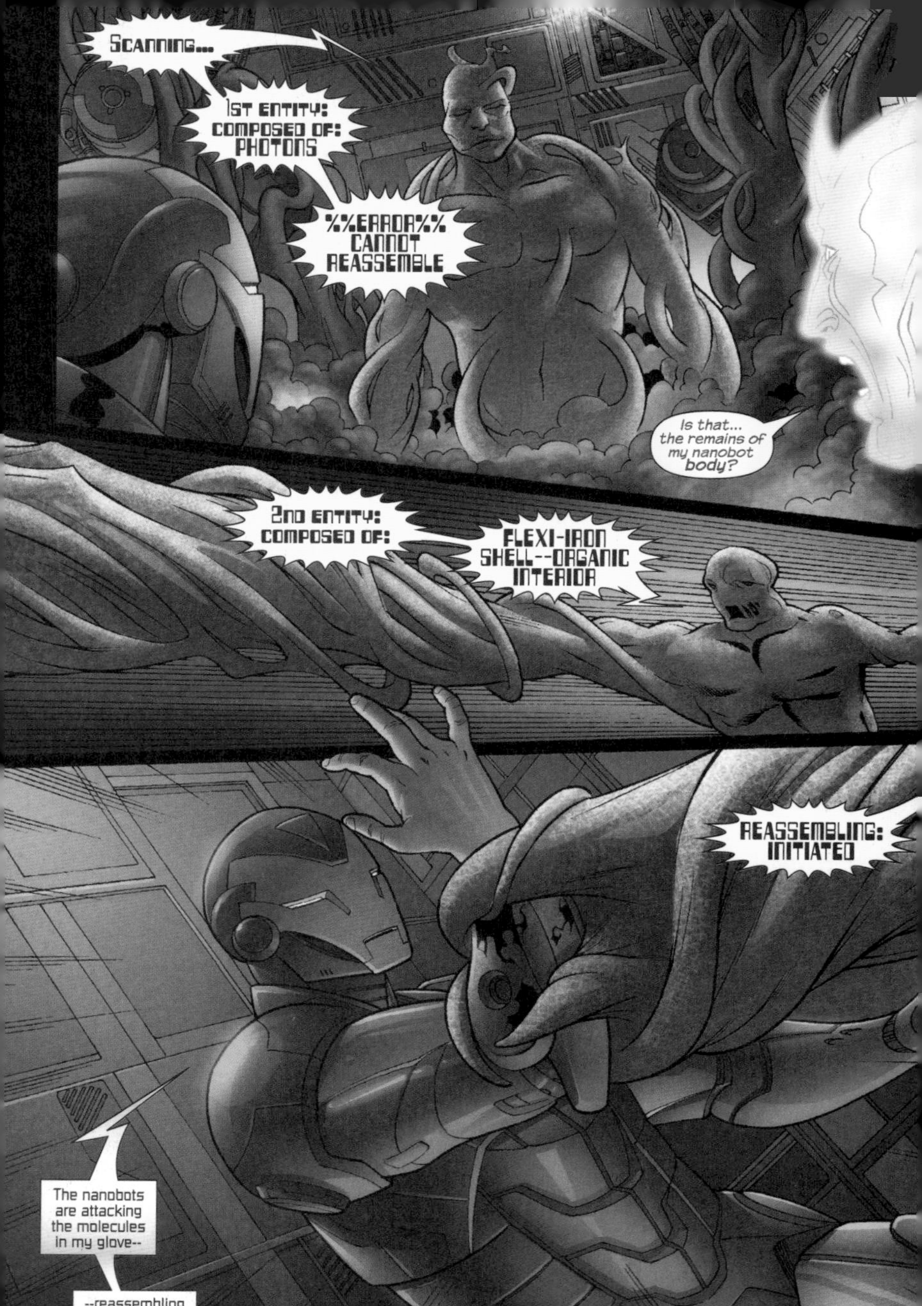
Scanning...
1st entity: composed of: photons
%%error%% cannot reassemble
Is that... the remains of my nanobot body?
2nd entity: composed of:
flexi-iron shell--organic interior
Reassembling: initiated
The nanobots are attacking the molecules in my glove--
--reassembling them into more nanobots!

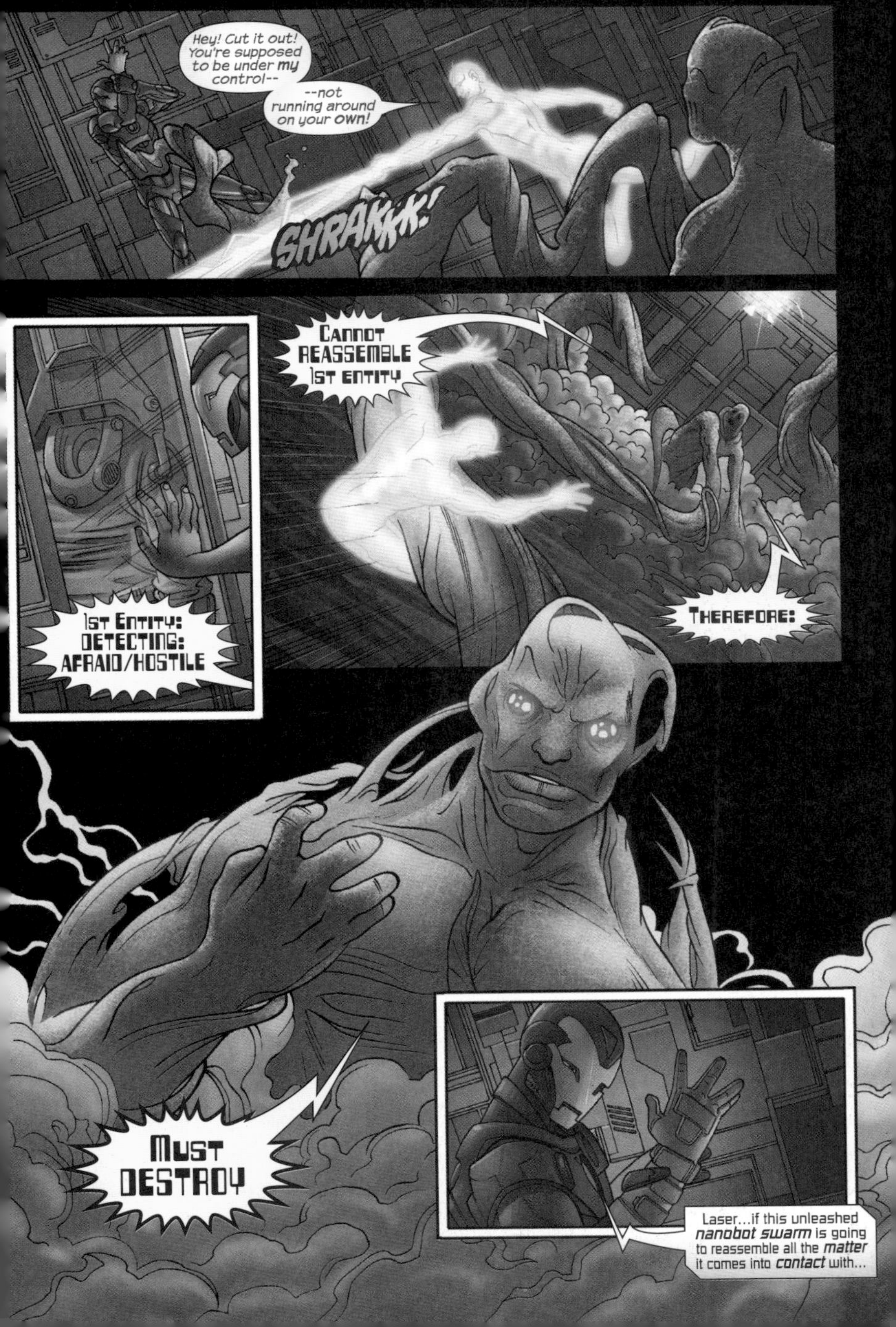

Hey! Cut it out! You're supposed to be under my control--
--not running around on your OWN!
SHRAKKK!
1st Entity: DETECTING: AFRAID/HOSTILE
Cannot REASSEMBLE 1st Entity
Therefore:
Must DESTROY
Laser...if this unleashed nanobot swarm is going to reassemble all the matter it comes into contact with...

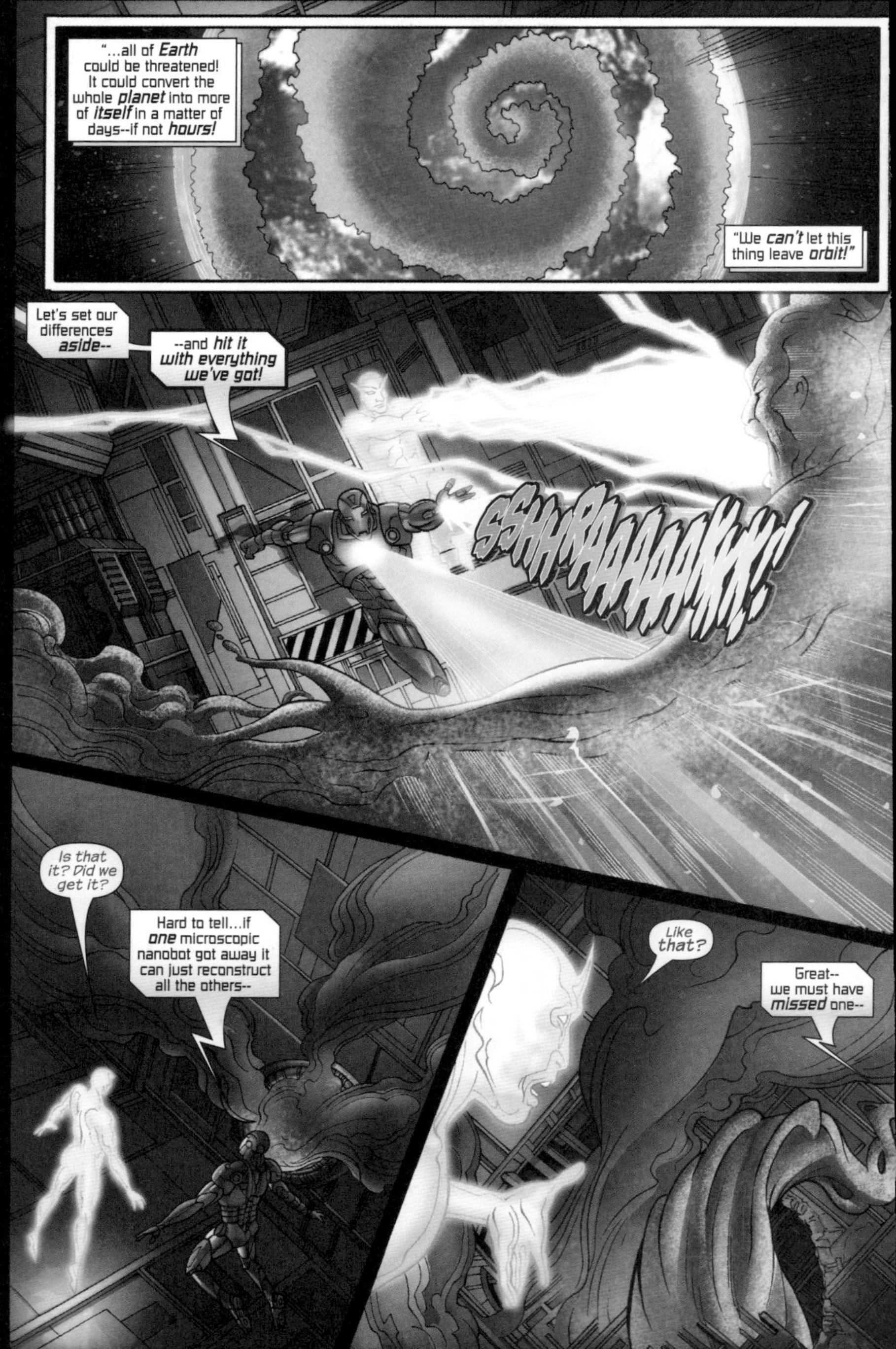
"...all of Earth could be threatened! It could convert the whole planet into more of itself in a matter of days--if not hours!
"We can't let this thing leave orbit!"
Let's set our differences aside--
--and hit it with everything we've got!
SSHHRAAAAAKK!!
Is that it? Did we get it?
Hard to tell...if one microscopic nanobot got away it can just reconstruct all the others--
Like that?
Great-- we must have missed one--

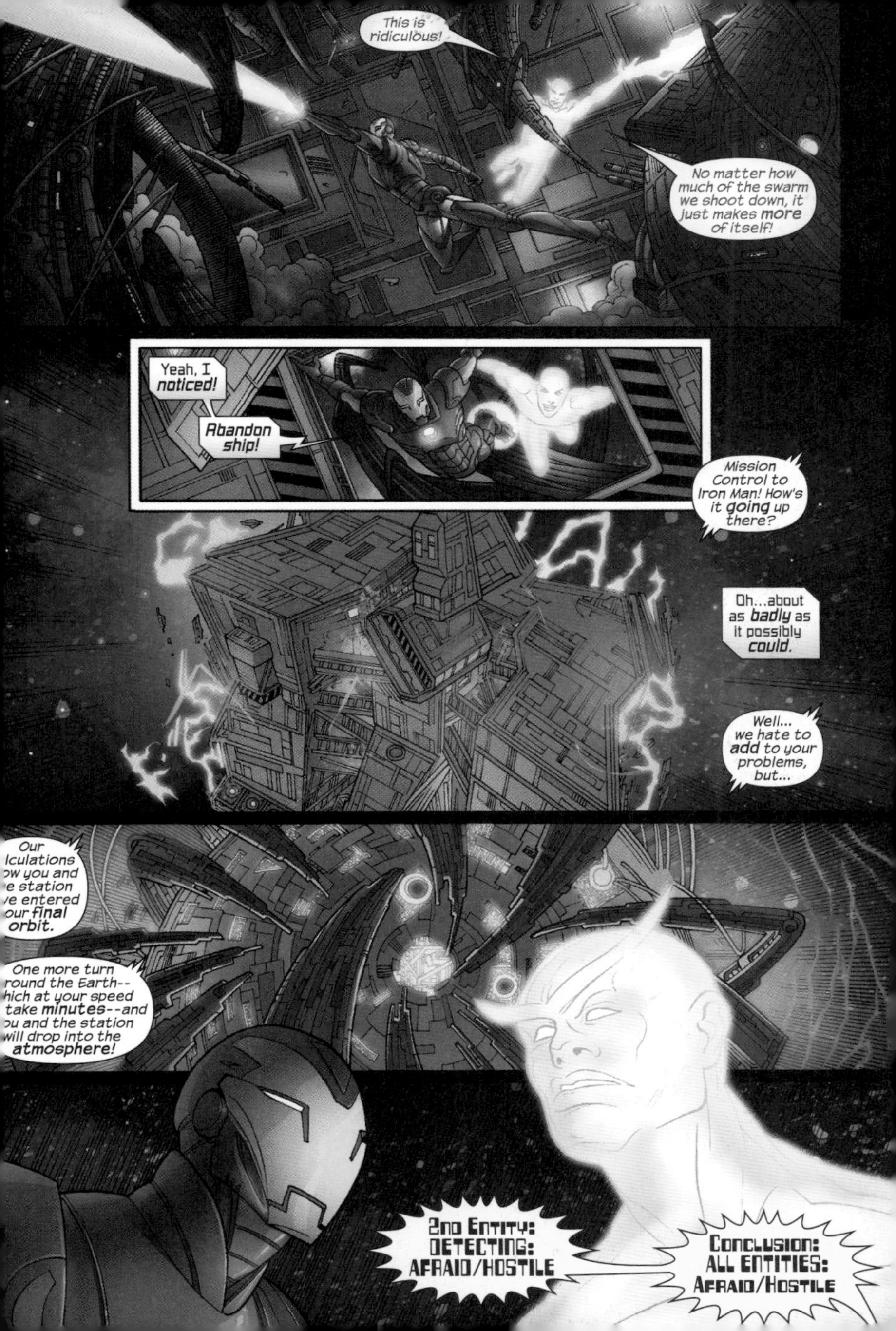
This is ridiculous!
No matter how much of the swarm we shoot down, it just makes more of itself!
Yeah, I noticed!
Abandon ship!
Mission Control to Iron Man! How's it going up there?
Oh...about as badly as it possibly could.
Well... we hate to add to your problems, but...
Our lculations ow you and e station ve entered our final orbit.
One more turn round the Earth-- hich at your speed take minutes--and ou and the station will drop into the atmosphere!
2nd Entity: Detecting: Afraid/Hostile
Conclusion: All Entities: Afraid/Hostile

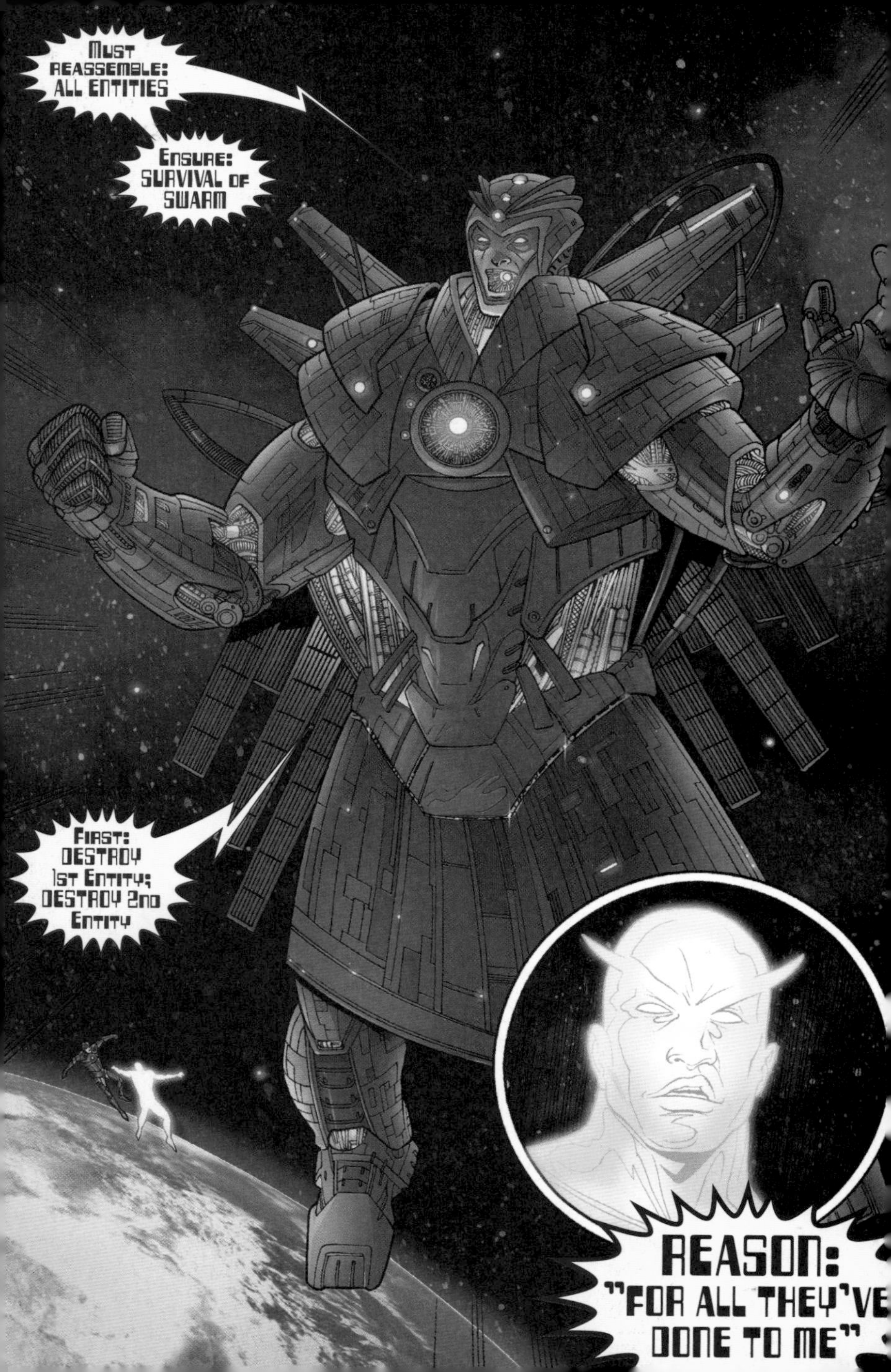
MUST REASSEMBLE: ALL ENTITIES
ENSURE: SURVIVAL OF SWARM
FIRST: DESTROY 1ST ENTITY; DESTROY 2ND ENTITY
REASON: "FOR ALL THEY'VE DONE TO ME"

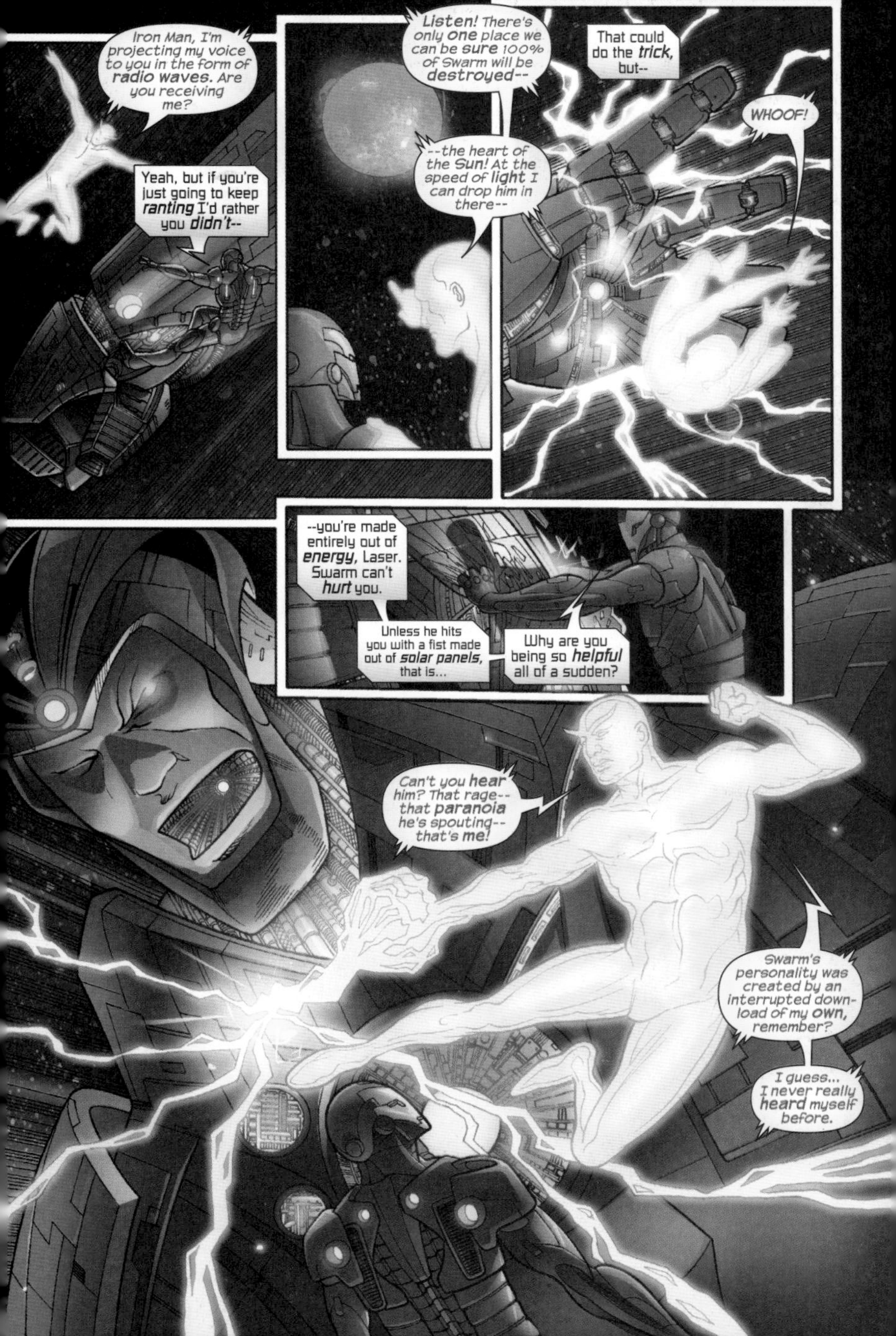
Iron Man, I'm projecting my voice to you in the form of radio waves. Are you receiving me?
Yeah, but if you're just going to keep ranting I'd rather you didn't--
Listen! There's only one place we can be sure 100% of Swarm will be destroyed--
--the heart of the Sun! At the speed of light I can drop him in there--
That could do the trick, but--
WHOOF!
--you're made entirely out of energy, Laser. Swarm can't hurt you.
Unless he hits you with a fist made out of solar panels, that is...
Why are you being so helpful all of a sudden?
Can't you hear him? That rage--that paranoia he's spouting--that's me!
Swarm's personality was created by an interrupted download of my own, remember?
I guess... I never really heard myself before.

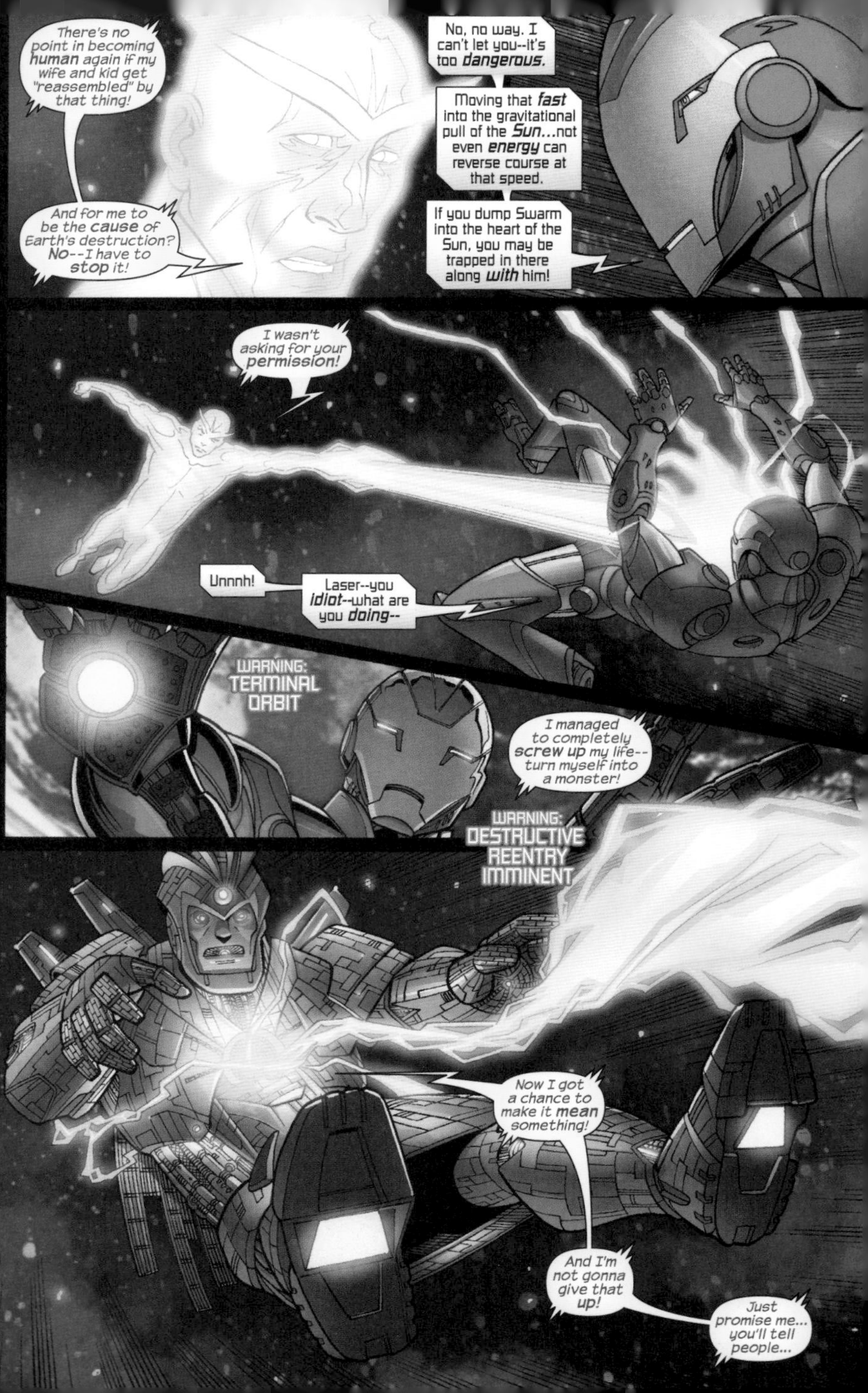
There's no point in becoming human again if my wife and kid get "reassembled" by that thing!
And for me to be the cause of Earth's destruction? No--I have to stop it!
No, no way. I can't let you--it's too dangerous.
Moving that fast into the gravitational pull of the Sun...not even energy can reverse course at that speed.
If you dump Swarm into the heart of the Sun, you may be trapped in there along with him!
I wasn't asking for your permission!
Unnnh!
Laser--you idiot--what are you doing--
WARNING: TERMINAL ORBIT
I managed to completely screw up my life--turn myself into a monster!
WARNING: DESTRUCTIVE REENTRY IMMINENT
Now I got a chance to make it mean something!
And I'm not gonna give that up!
Just promise me... you'll tell people...

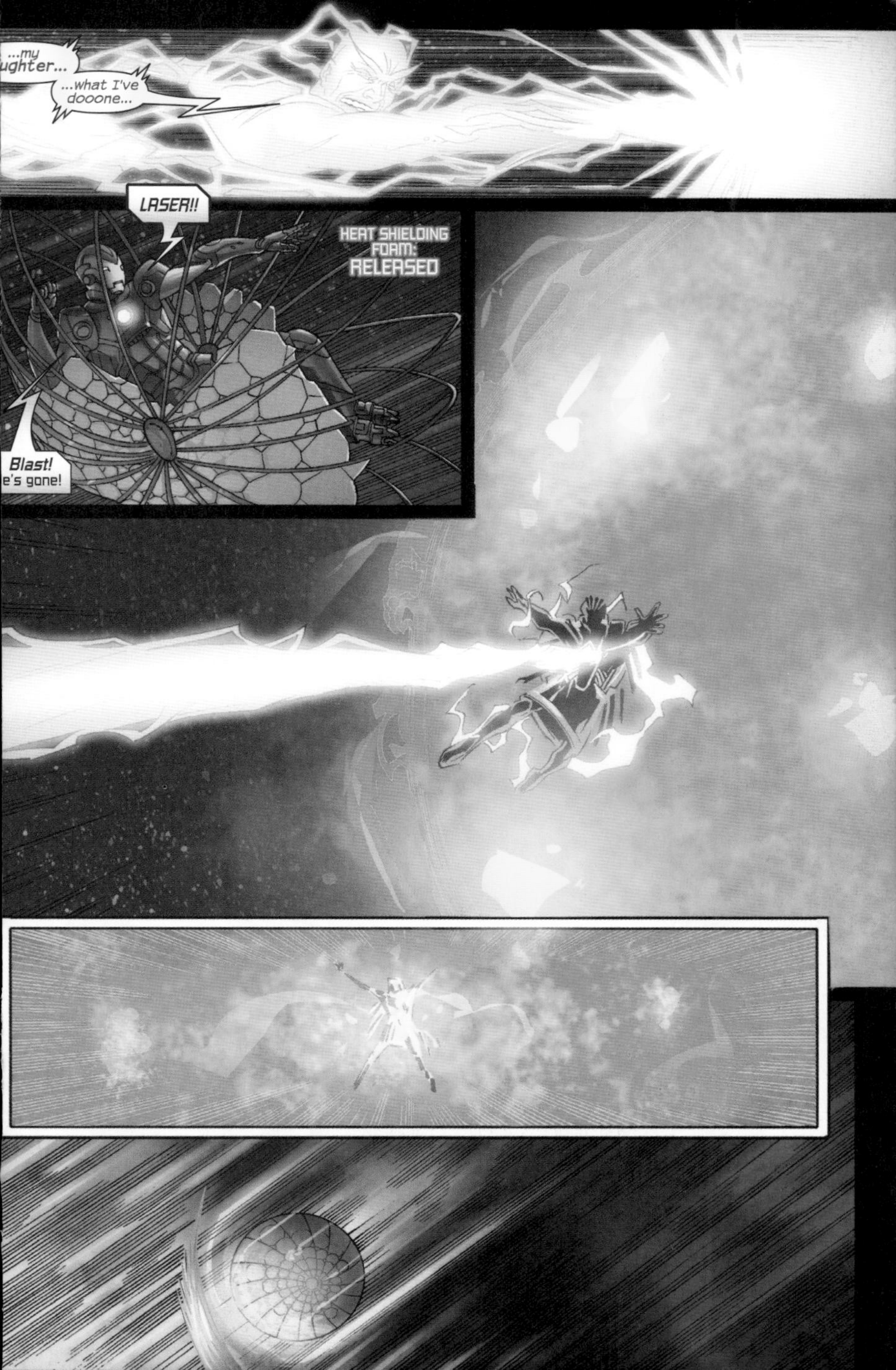

...my ughter...
...what I've dooone...
LASER!!
HEAT SHIELDING FOAM: RELEASED
Blast! e's gone!

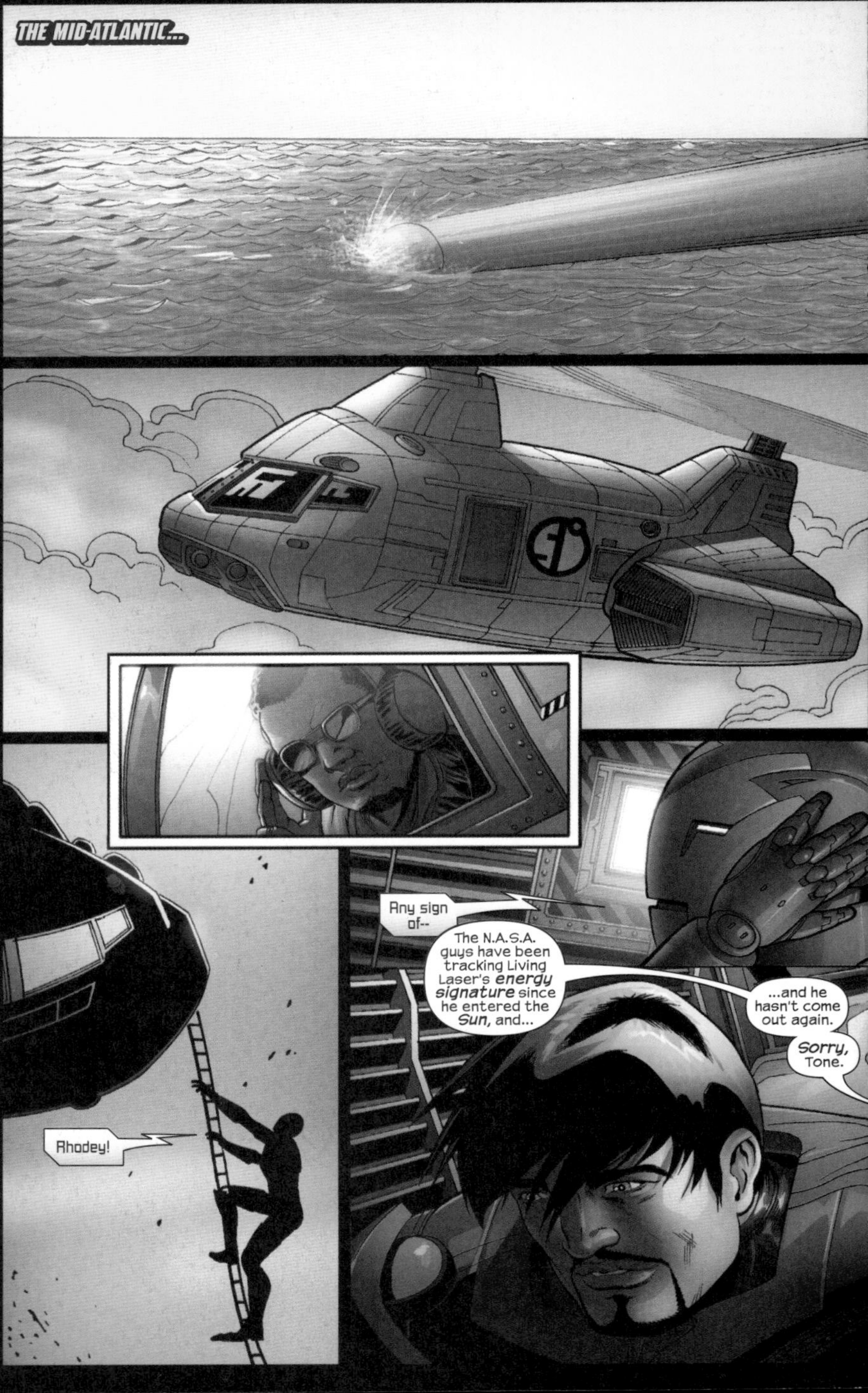
THE MID-ATLANTIC...
Any sign of--
The N.A.S.A. guys have been tracking Living Laser's energy signature since he entered the Sun, and...
...and he hasn't come out again.
Sorry, Tone.
Rhodey!

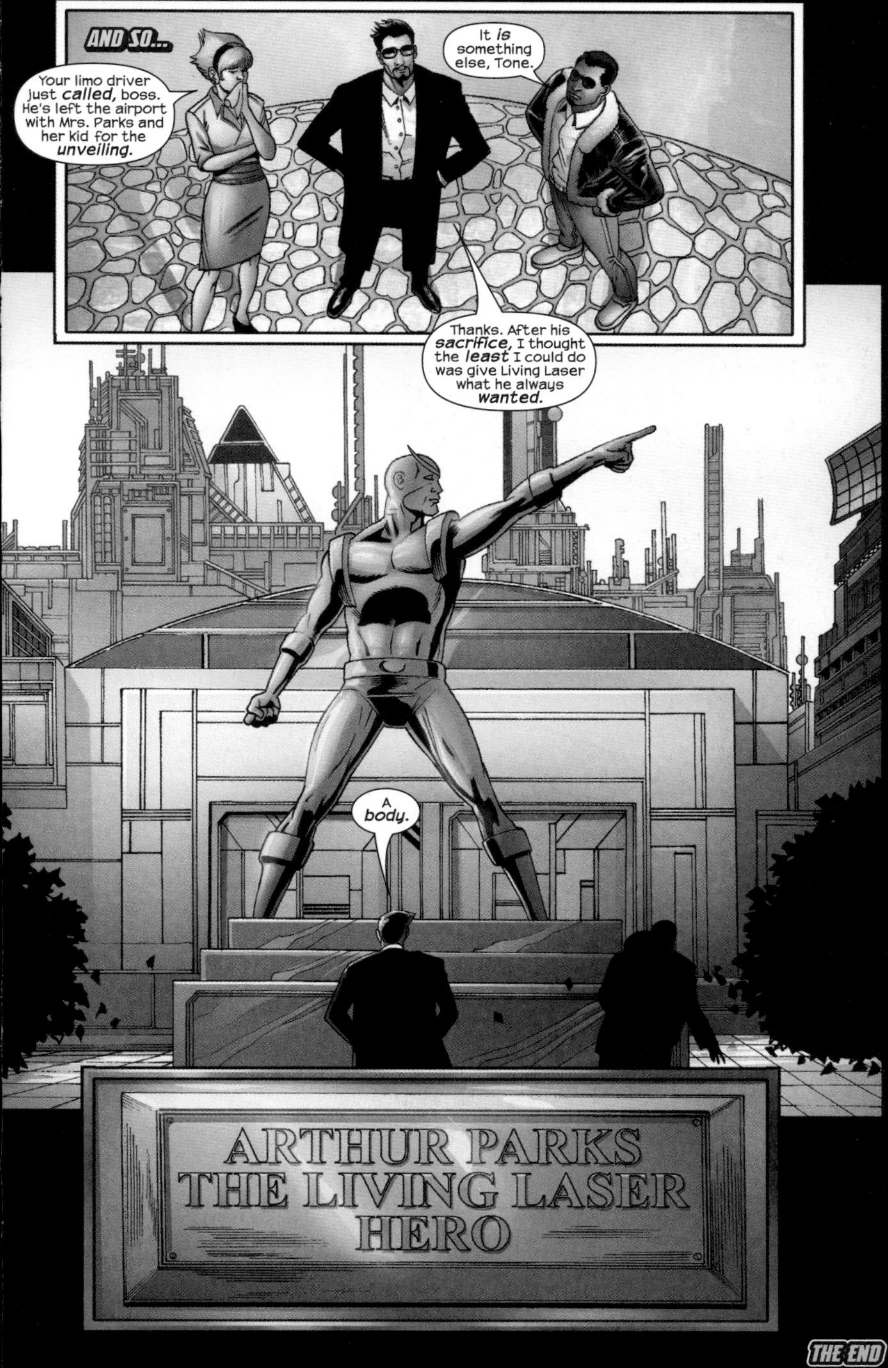
AND SO...
Your limo driver just called, boss. He's left the airport with Mrs. Parks and her kid for the unveiling.
It is something else, Tone.
Thanks. After his sacrifice, I thought the least I could do was give Living Laser what he always wanted.
A body.
ARTHUR PARKS
THE LIVING LASER
HERO
THE END

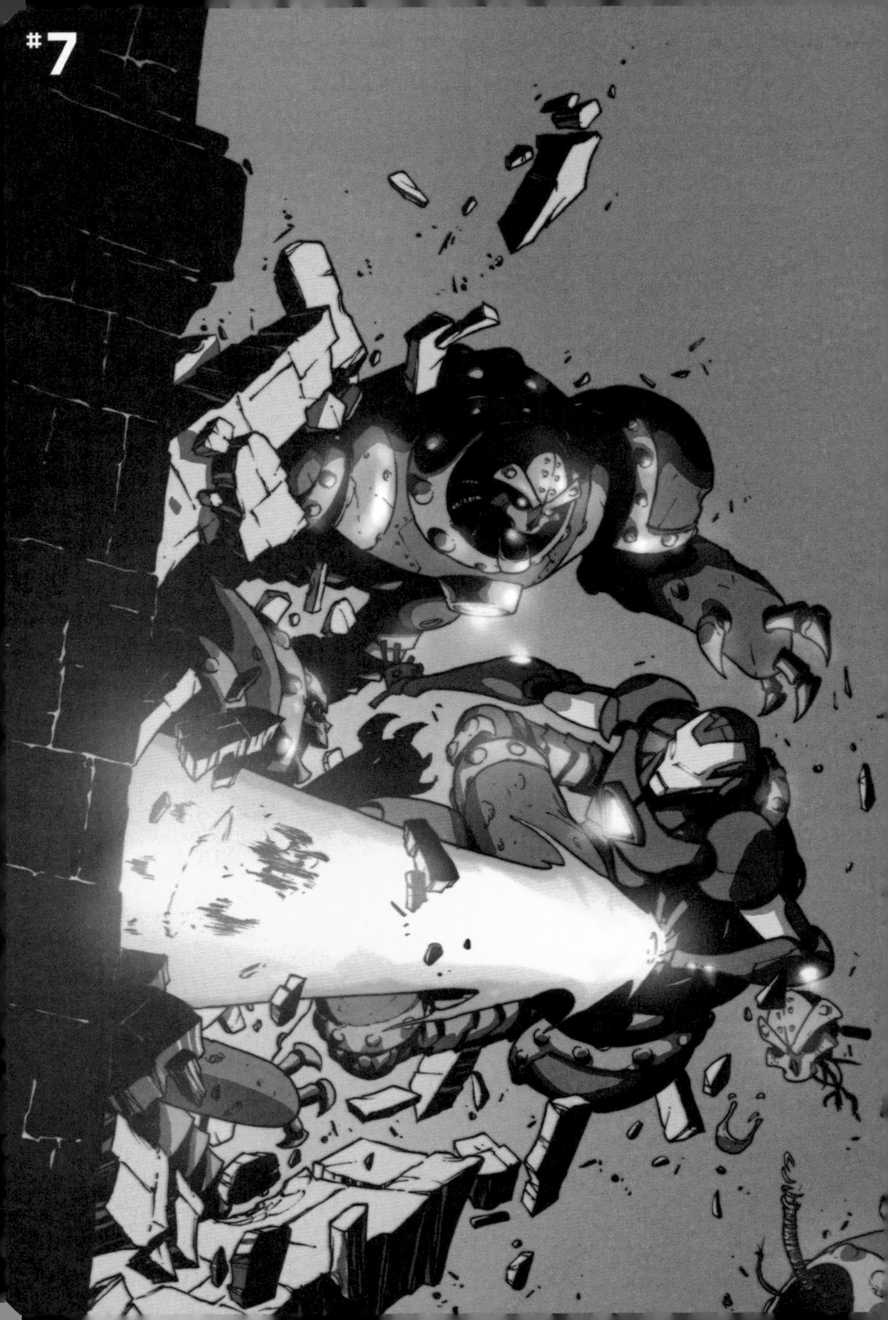
#7

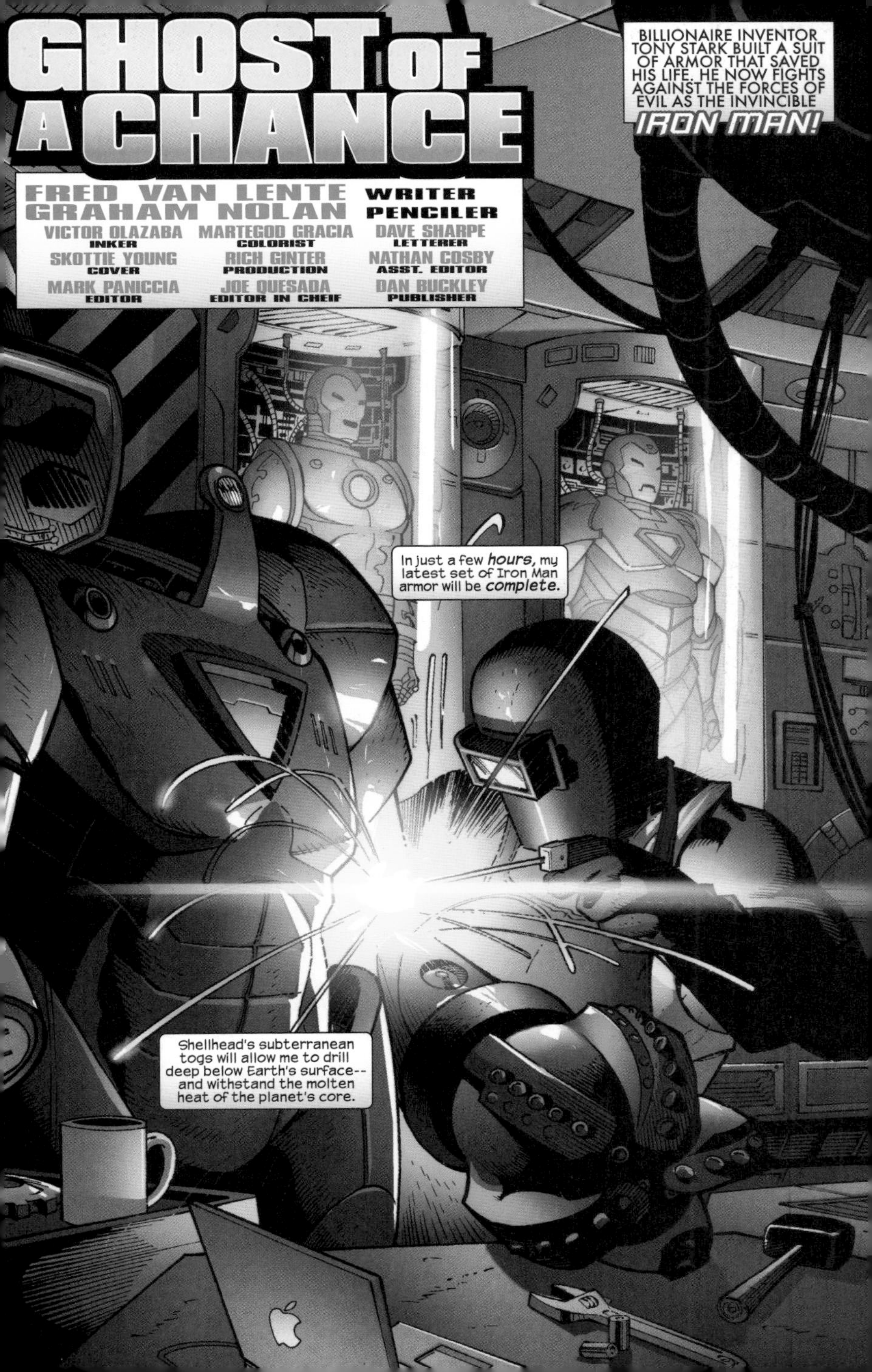
GHOST OF A CHANCE
FRED VAN LENTE WRITER
GRAHAM NOLAN PENCILER
VICTOR OLAZABA INKER
MARTEGOD GRACIA COLORIST
DAVE SHARPE LETTERER
SKOTTIE YOUNG COVER
RICH GINTER PRODUCTION
NATHAN COSBY ASST. EDITOR
MARK PANICCIA EDITOR
JOE QUESADA EDITOR IN CHEIF
DAN BUCKLEY PUBLISHER
BILLIONAIRE INVENTOR TONY STARK BUILT A SUIT OF ARMOR THAT SAVED HIS LIFE. HE NOW FIGHTS AGAINST THE FORCES OF EVIL AS THE INVINCIBLE IRON MAN!
In just a few *hours,* my latest set of Iron Man armor will be *complete.*
Shellhead's subterranean togs will allow me to drill deep below Earth's surface--and withstand the molten heat of the planet's core.

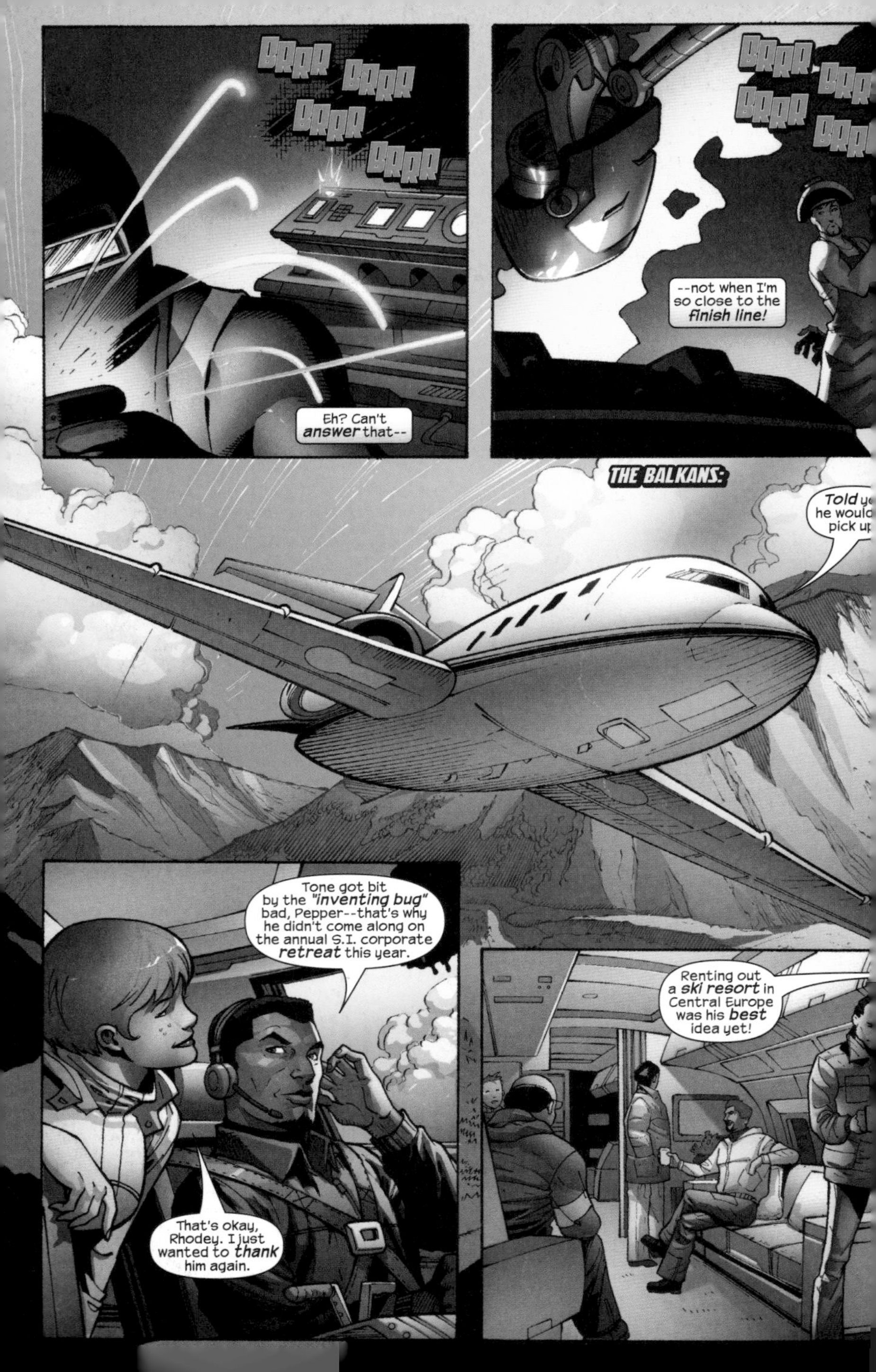
BRRR BRRR BRRR BRRR
Eh? Can't answer that--
BRRR BRRR BRRR
--not when I'm so close to the finish line!
THE BALKANS:
Tone got bit by the "inventing bug" bad, Pepper--that's why he didn't come along on the annual S.I. corporate retreat this year.
That's okay, Rhodey. I just wanted to thank him again.
Renting out a ski resort in Central Europe was his best idea yet!

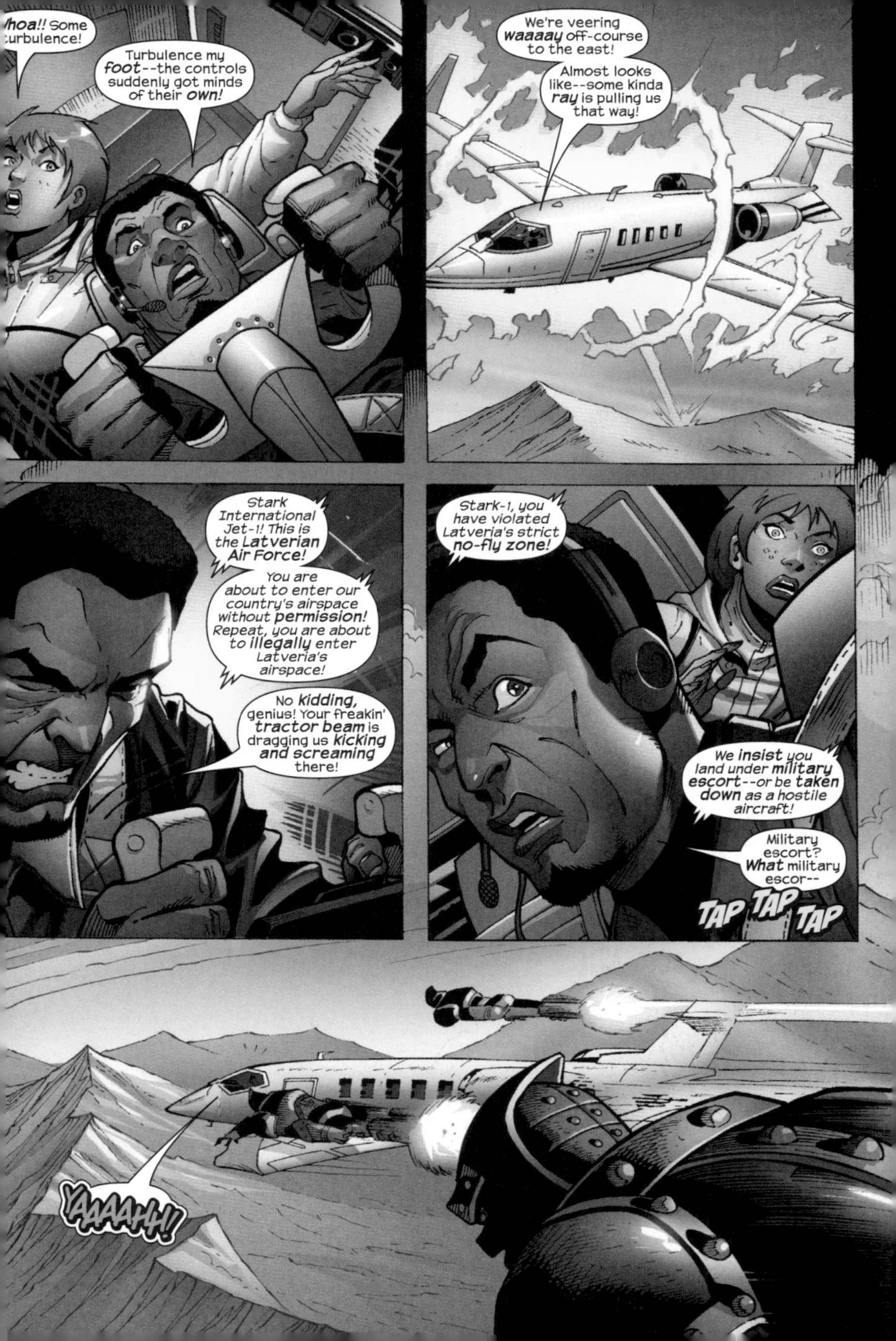
Whoa!! Some turbulence!
Turbulence my foot--the controls suddenly got minds of their own!
We're veering waaaay off-course to the east!
Almost looks like--some kinda ray is pulling us that way!
Stark International Jet-1! This is the Latverian Air Force!
You are about to enter our country's airspace without permission! Repeat, you are about to illegally enter Latveria's airspace!
No kidding, genius! Your freakin' tractor beam is dragging us kicking and screaming there!
Stark-1, you have violated Latveria's strict no-fly zone!
We insist you land under military escort--or be taken down as a hostile aircraft!
Military escort? What military escor--
TAP TAP TAP
YAAAAHH!!

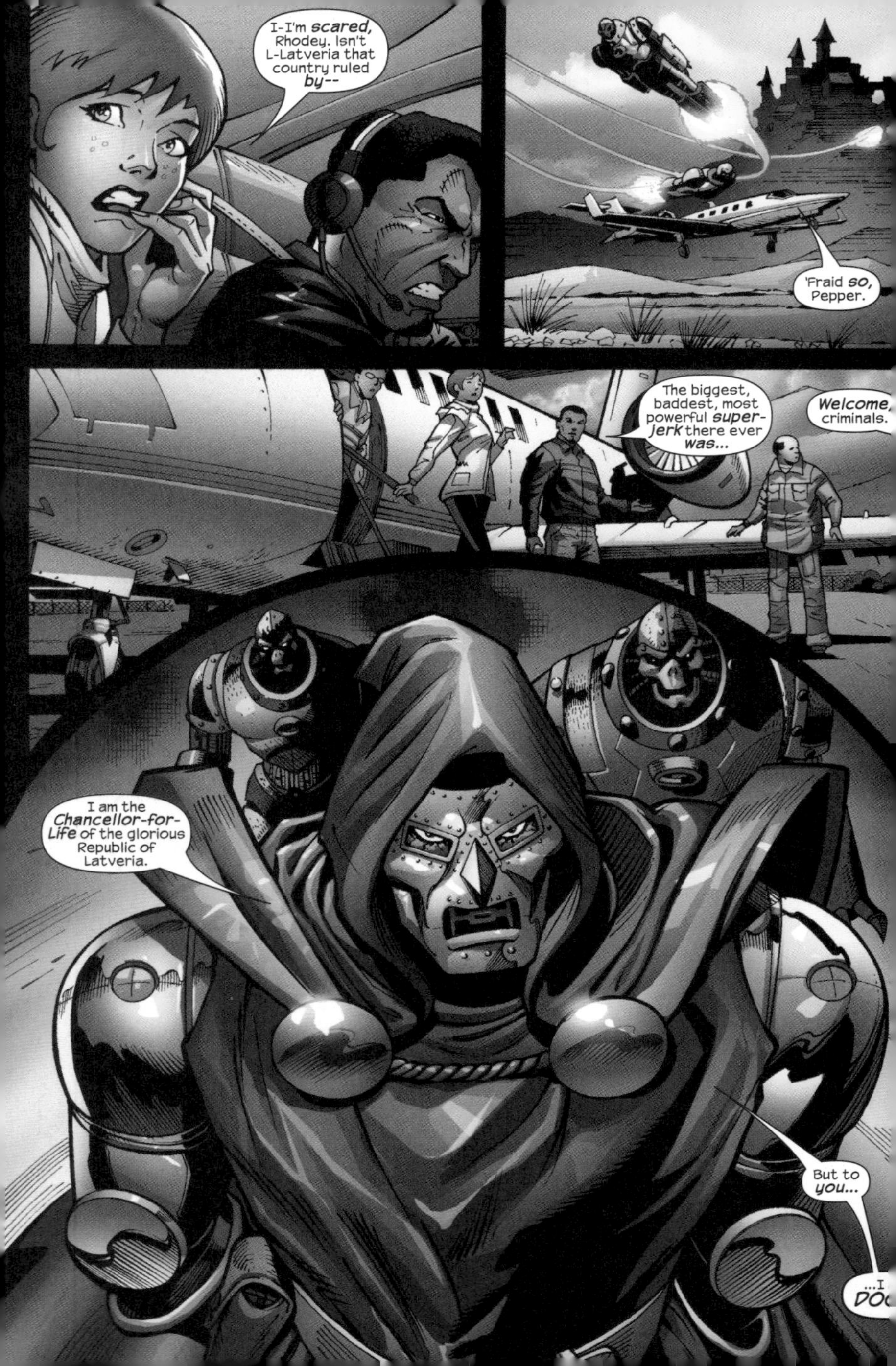
I-I'm scared, Rhodey. Isn't L-Latveria that country ruled by--
'Fraid so, Pepper.
The biggest, baddest, most powerful super-jerk there ever was...
Welcome, criminals.
I am the Chancellor-for-Life of the glorious Republic of Latveria.
But to you...
...I DO

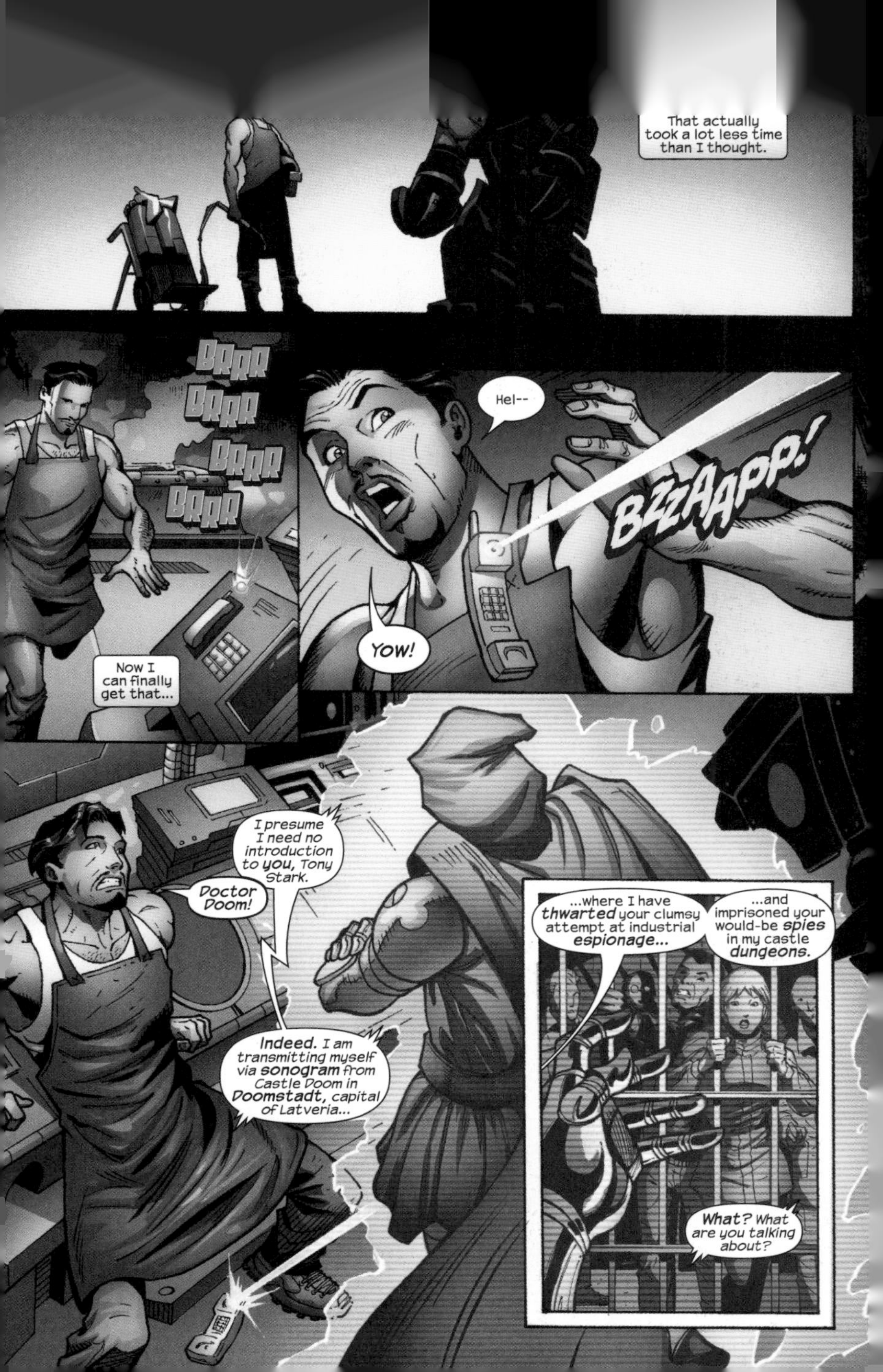

That actually took a lot less time than I thought.
BRRR BRRR BRRR BRRR
Now I can finally get that...
Hel--
BZZAAPP!
YOW!
I presume I need no introduction to you, Tony Stark.
Doctor Doom!
Indeed. I am transmitting myself via sonogram from Castle Doom in Doomstadt, capital of Latveria...
...where I have thwarted your clumsy attempt at industrial espionage...
...and imprisoned your would-be spies in my castle dungeons.
What? What are you talking about?

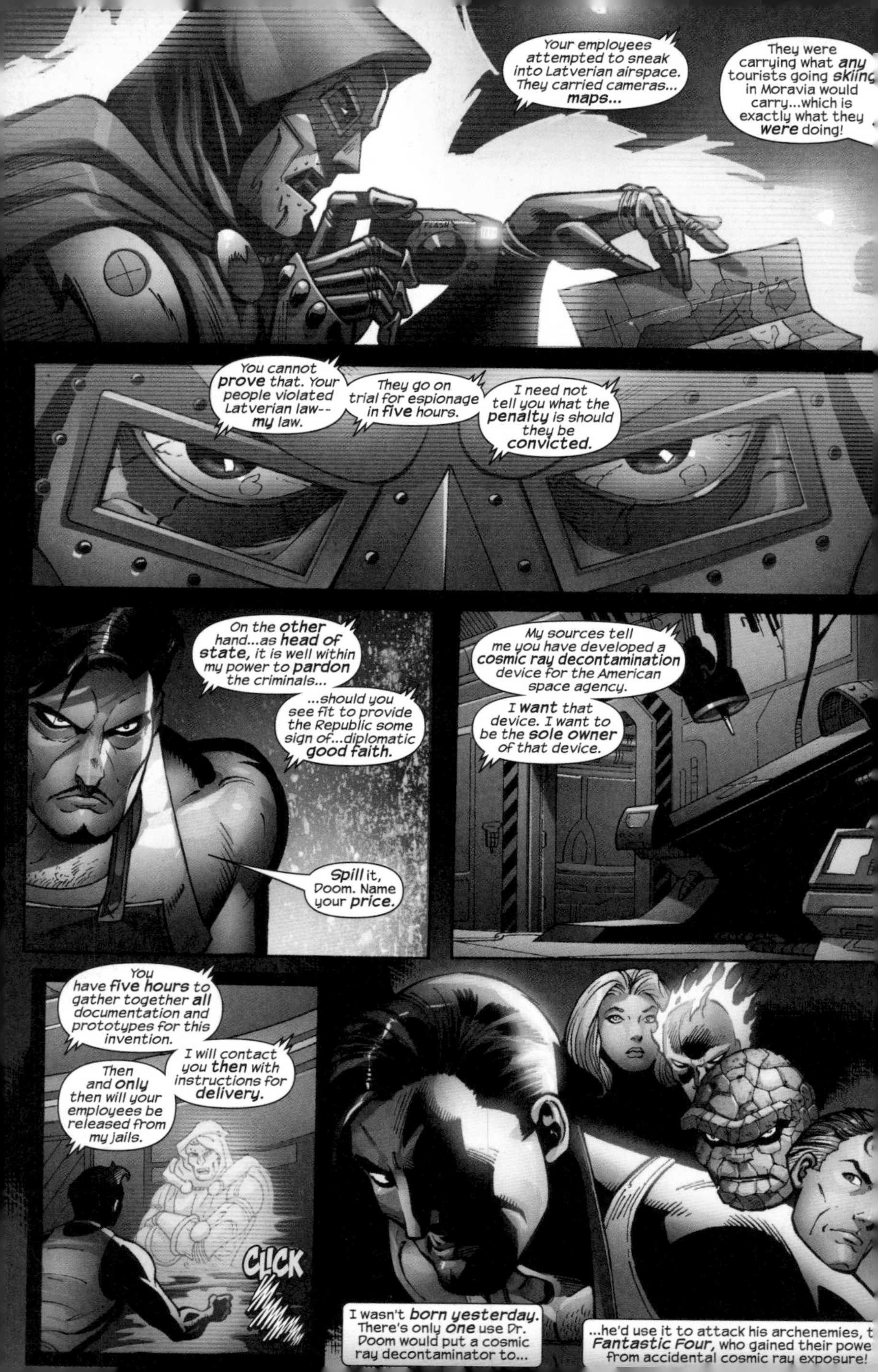
Your employees attempted to sneak into Latverian airspace. They carried cameras... maps...
They were carrying what any tourists going skiing in Moravia would carry...which is exactly what they were doing!
You cannot prove that. Your people violated Latverian law-- my law.
They go on trial for espionage in five hours.
I need not tell you what the penalty is should they be convicted.
On the other hand...as head of state, it is well within my power to pardon the criminals...
...should you see fit to provide the Republic some sign of...diplomatic good faith.
Spill it, Doom. Name your price.
My sources tell me you have developed a cosmic ray decontamination device for the American space agency.
I want that device. I want to be the sole owner of that device.
You have five hours to gather together all documentation and prototypes for this invention.
I will contact you then with instructions for delivery.
Then and only then will your employees be released from my jails.
CLICK
I wasn't born yesterday. There's only one use Dr. Doom would put a cosmic ray decontaminator to...
...he'd use it to attack his archenemies, t Fantastic Four, who gained their powe from accidental cosmic ray exposure!

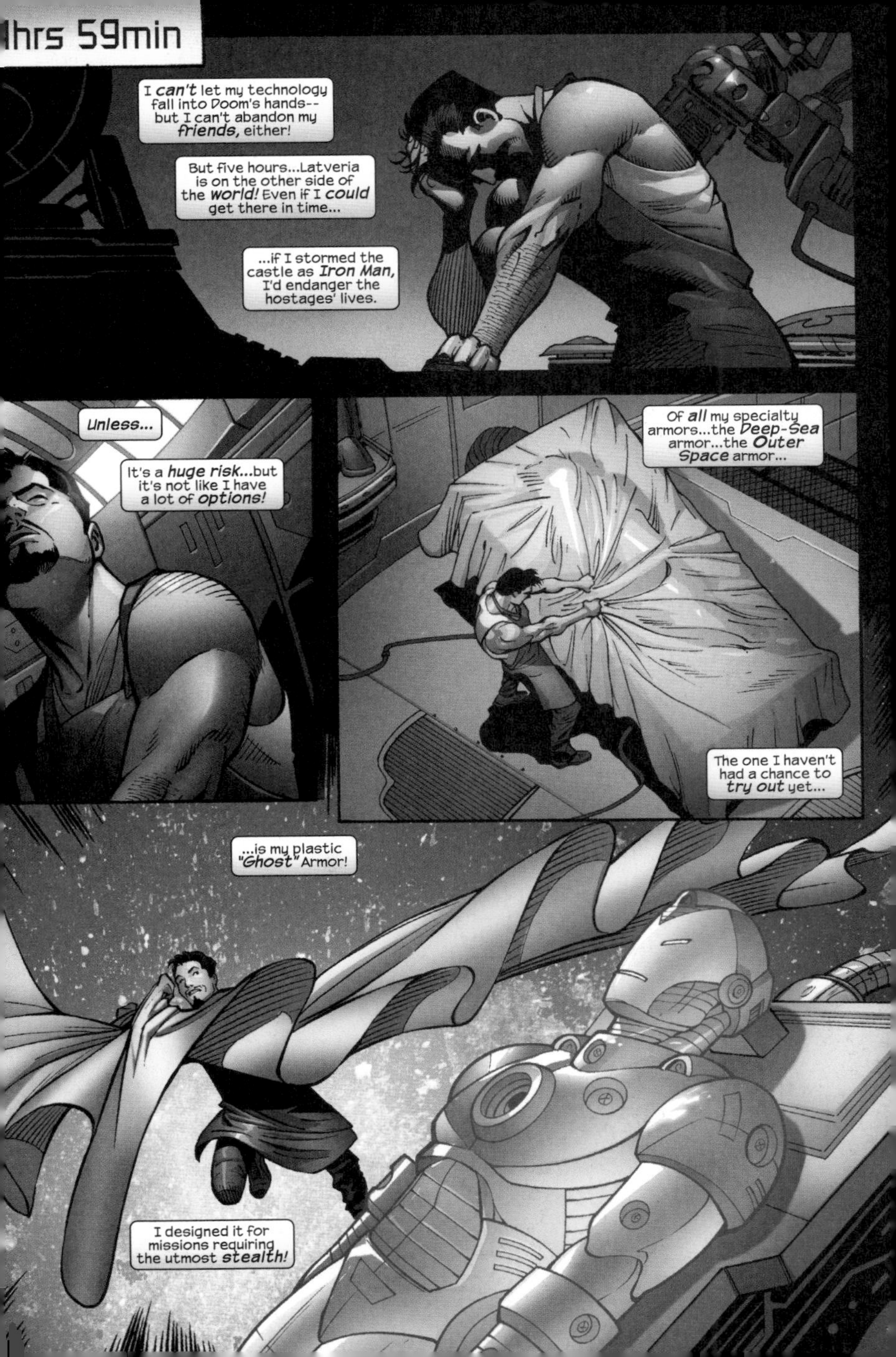
hrs 59min
I can't let my technology fall into Doom's hands-- but I can't abandon my friends, either!
But five hours...Latveria is on the other side of the world! Even if I could get there in time...
...if I stormed the castle as Iron Man, I'd endanger the hostages' lives.
Unless...
It's a huge risk...but it's not like I have a lot of options!
Of all my specialty armors...the Deep-Sea armor...the Outer Space armor...
The one I haven't had a chance to try out yet...
...is my plastic "Ghost" Armor!
I designed it for missions requiring the utmost stealth!

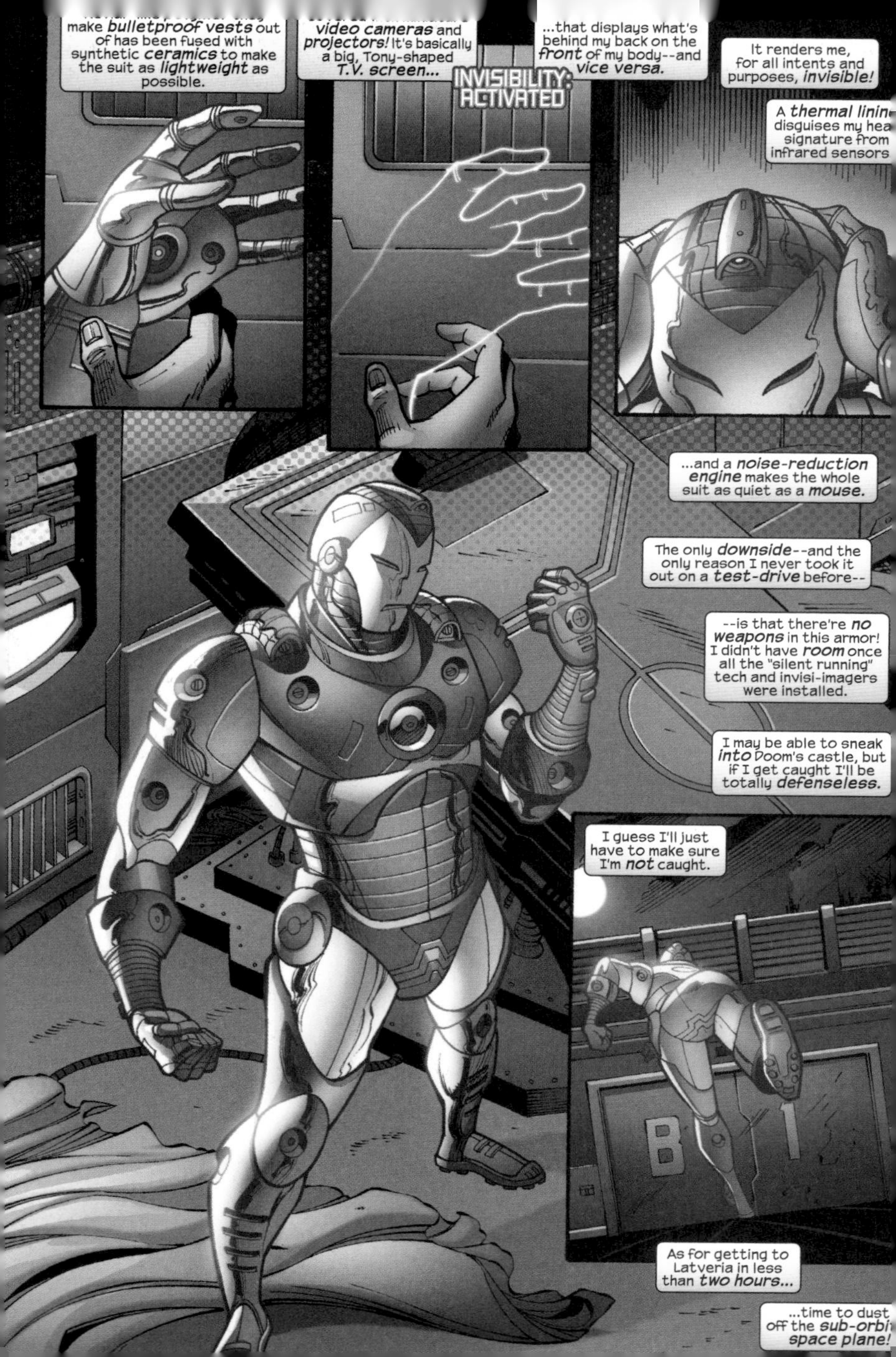
make bulletproof vests out of has been fused with synthetic ceramics to make the suit as lightweight as possible.
video cameras and projectors! It's basically a big, Tony-shaped T.V. screen...
INVISIBILITY: ACTIVATED
...that displays what's behind my back on the front of my body--and vice versa.
It renders me, for all intents and purposes, invisible!
A thermal linin disguises my hea signature from infrared sensors
...and a noise-reduction engine makes the whole suit as quiet as a mouse.
The only downside--and the only reason I never took it out on a test-drive before--
--is that there're no weapons in this armor! I didn't have room once all the "silent running" tech and invisi-imagers were installed.
I may be able to sneak into Doom's castle, but if I get caught I'll be totally defenseless.
I guess I'll just have to make sure I'm not caught.
B 1
As for getting to Latveria in less than two hours...
...time to dust off the sub-orbi space plane!

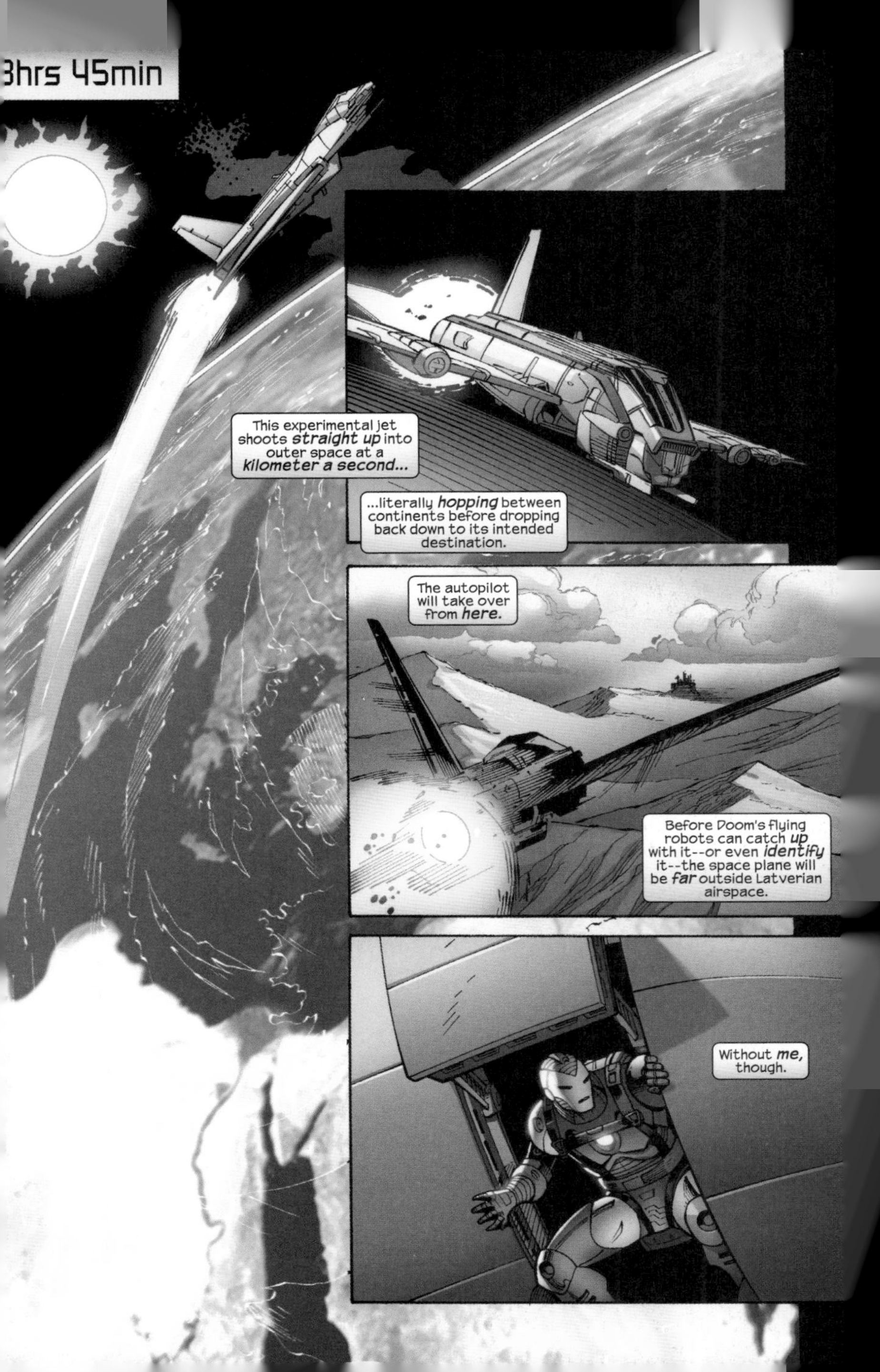
3hrs 45min
This experimental jet shoots straight up into outer space at a kilometer a second...
...literally hopping between continents before dropping back down to its intended destination.
The autopilot will take over from here.
Before Doom's flying robots can catch up with it--or even identify it--the space plane will be far outside Latverian airspace.
Without me, though.

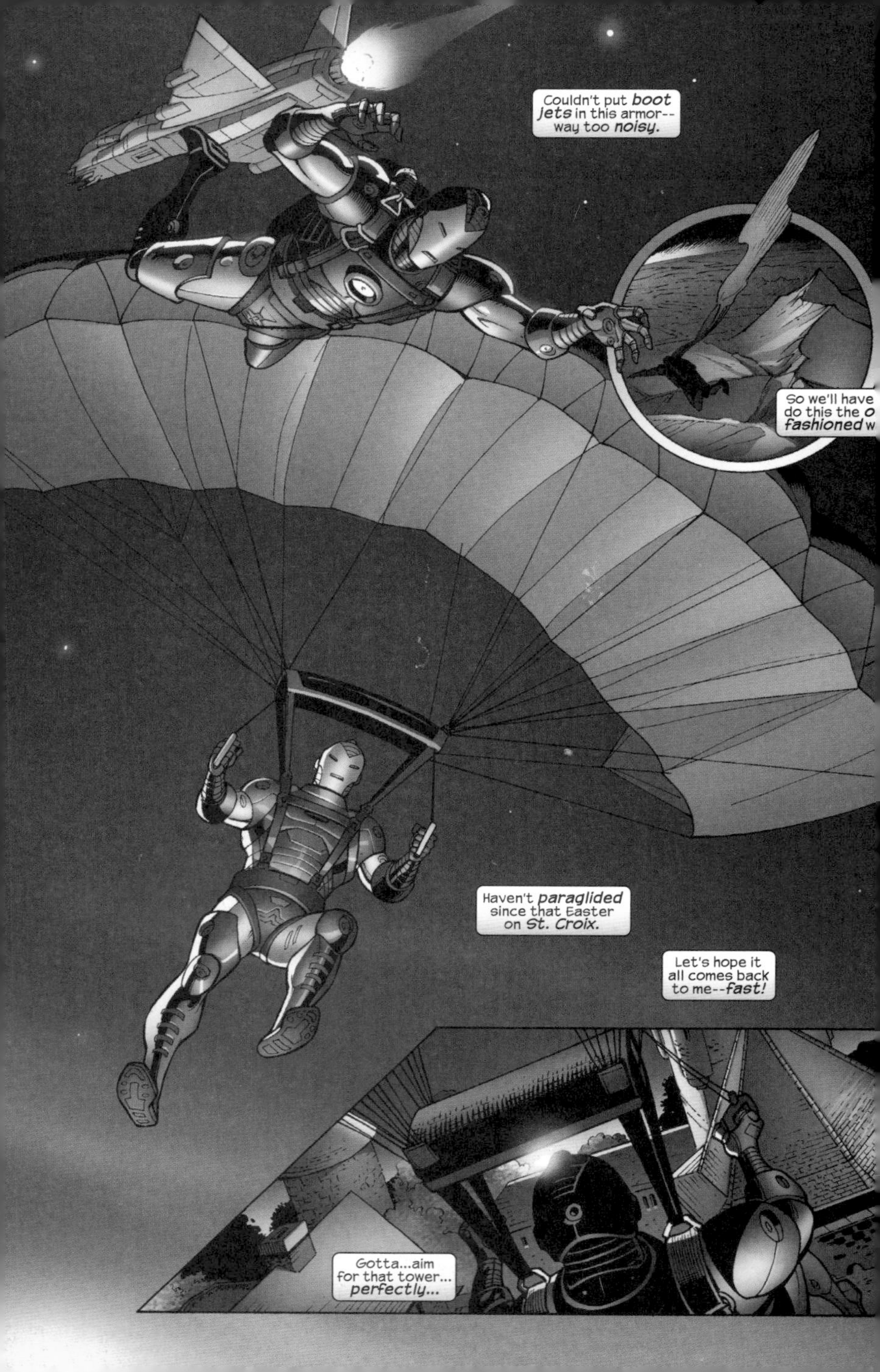

Couldn't put boot jets in this armor-- way too noisy.
So we'll have do this the o fashioned w
Haven't paraglided since that Easter on St. Croix.
Let's hope it all comes back to me--fast!
Gotta...aim for that tower... perfectly...

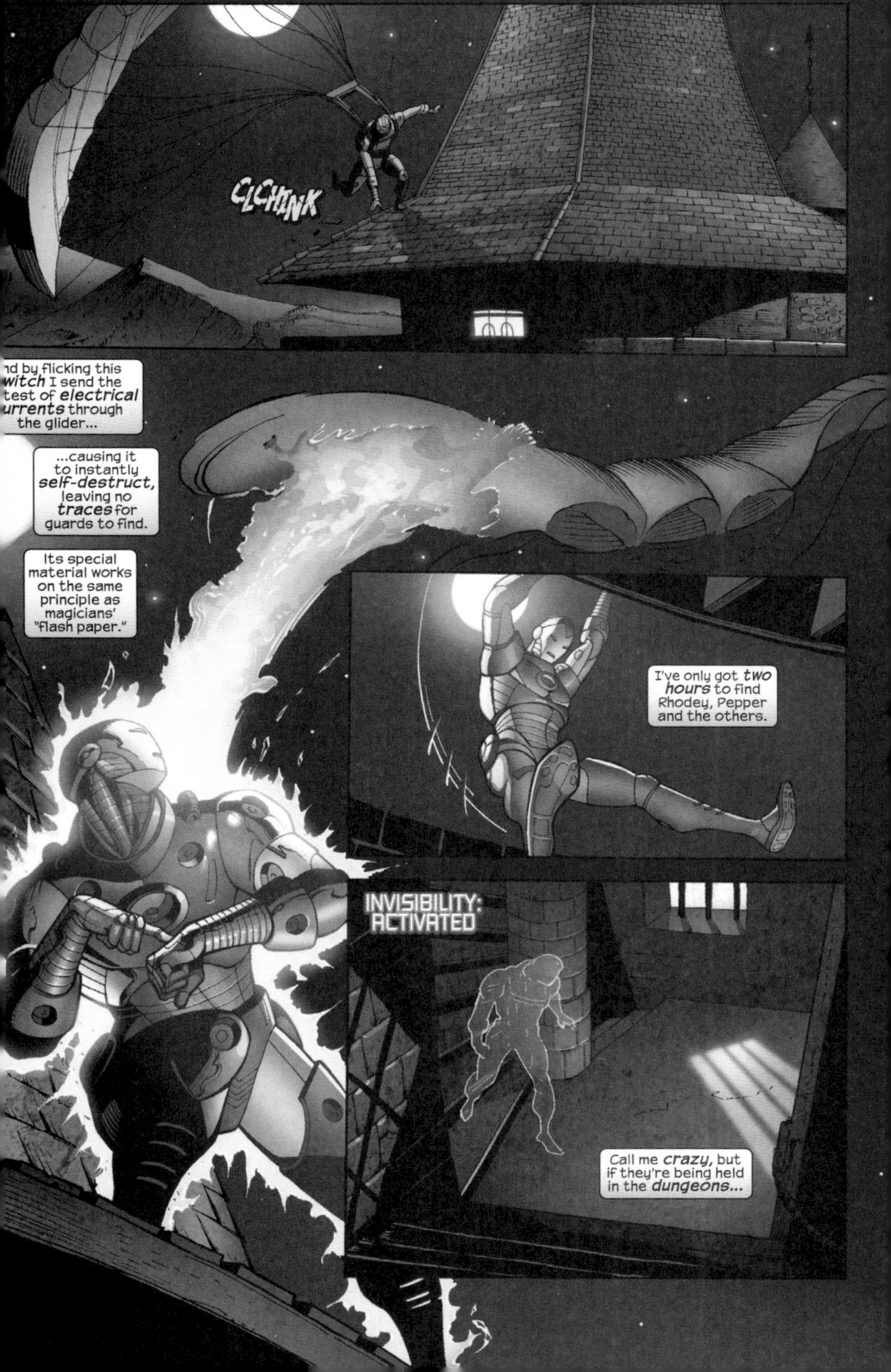
CLCHINK
nd by flicking this witch I send the test of electrical urrents through the glider...
...causing it to instantly self-destruct, leaving no traces for guards to find.
Its special material works on the same principle as magicians' "flash paper."
I've only got two hours to find Rhodey, Pepper and the others.
INVISIBILITY: ACTIVATED
Call me crazy, but if they're being held in the dungeons...

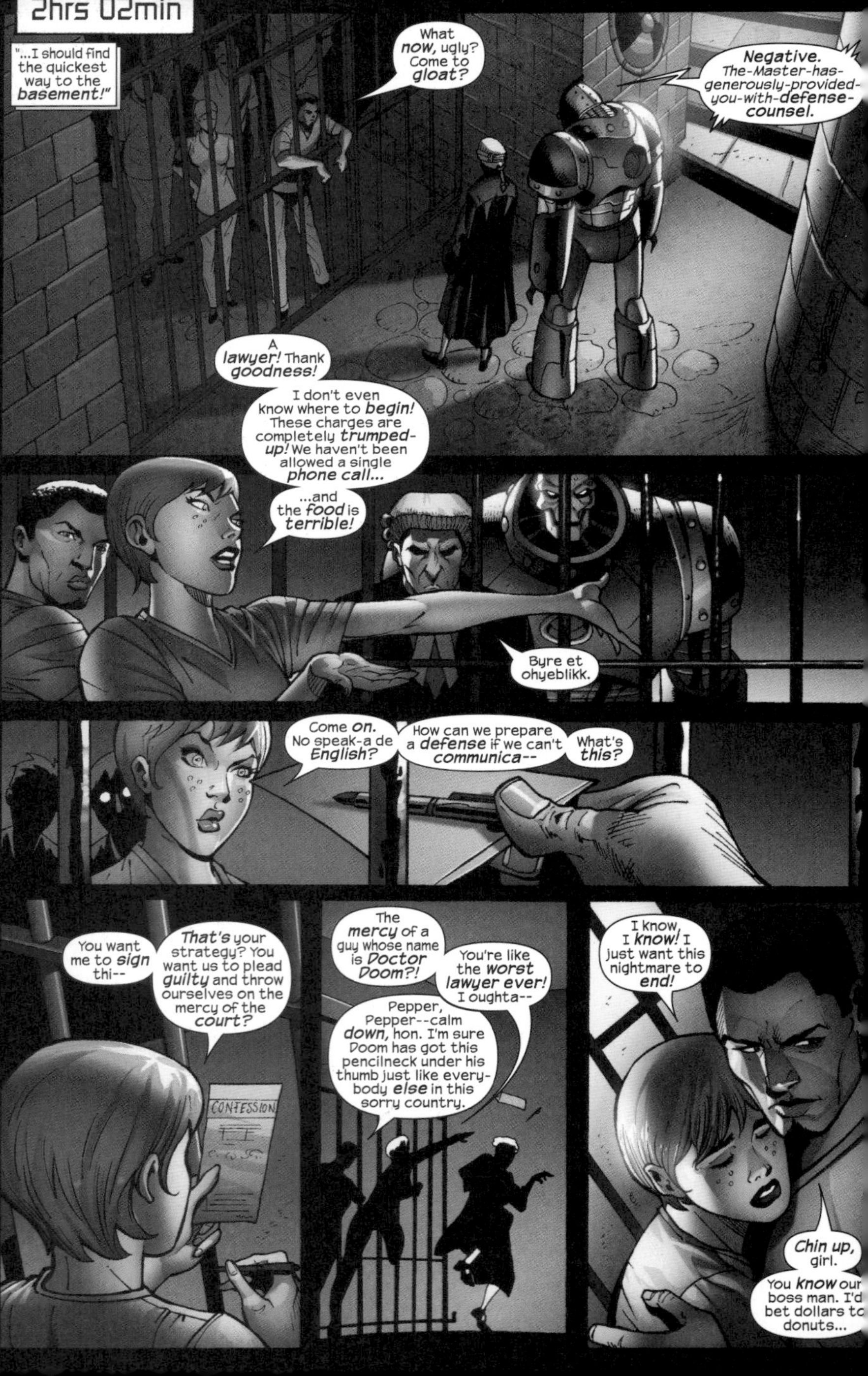
2hrs 02min
"...I should find the quickest way to the basement!"
What now, ugly? Come to gloat?
Negative. The-Master-has-generously-provided-you-with-defense-counsel.
A lawyer! Thank goodness!
I don't even know where to begin! These charges are completely trumped-up! We haven't been allowed a single phone call...
...and the food is terrible!
Byre et ohyeblikk.
Come on. No speak-a de English?
How can we prepare a defense if we can't communica--
What's this?
You want me to sign thi--
That's your strategy? You want us to plead guilty and throw ourselves on the mercy of the court?
CONFESSION
The mercy of a guy whose name is Doctor Doom?!
You're like the worst lawyer ever! I oughta--
Pepper, Pepper--calm down, hon. I'm sure Doom has got this pencilneck under his thumb just like every-body else in this sorry country.
I know, I know! I just want this nightmare to end!
Chin up, girl.
You know our boss man. I'd bet dollars to donuts...

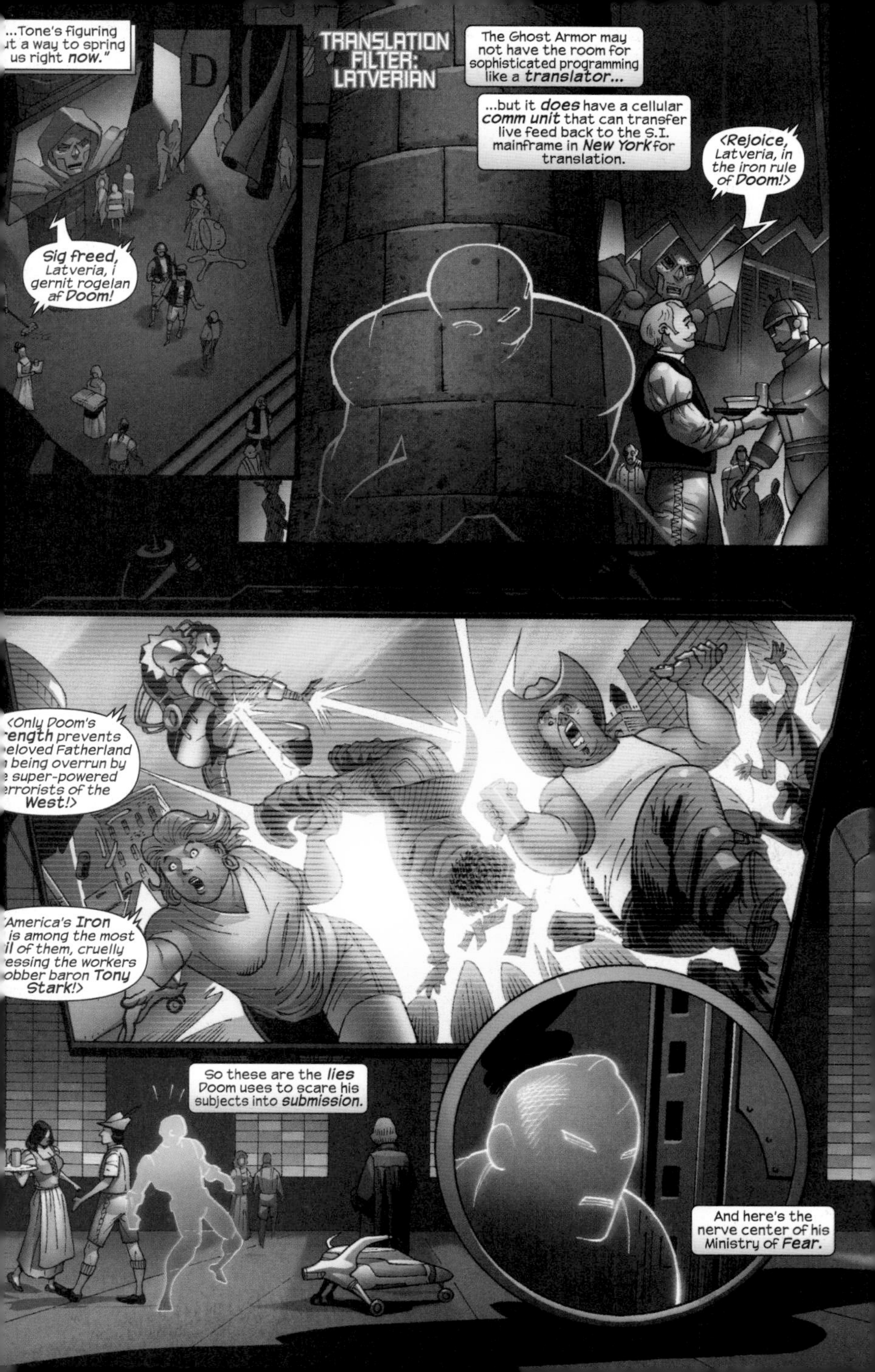

...Tone's figuring
ut a way to spring
us right now."
TRANSLATION FILTER: LATVERIAN
The Ghost Armor may not have the room for sophisticated programming like a translator...
...but it does have a cellular comm unit that can transfer live feed back to the S.I. mainframe in New York for translation.
Sig freed, Latveria, i gernit rogelan af Doom!
<Rejoice, Latveria, in the iron rule of Doom!>
<Only Doom's
rength prevents
eloved Fatherland
being overrun by
e super-powered
errorists of the
West!>
"America's Iron
is among the most
il of them, cruelly
essing the workers
obber baron Tony
Stark!>
So these are the lies Doom uses to scare his subjects into submission.
And here's the nerve center of his Ministry of Fear.

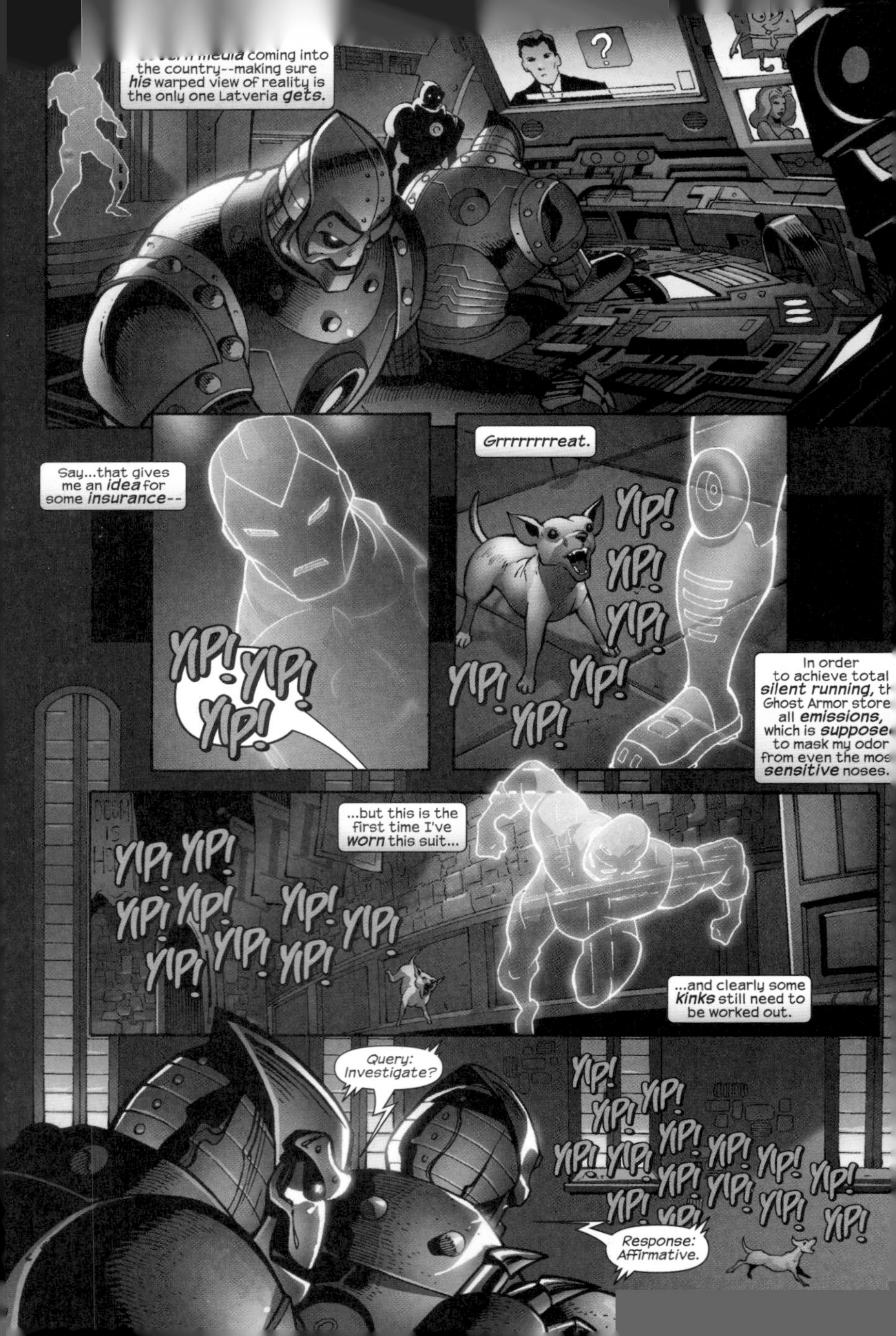
media coming into the country--making sure his warped view of reality is the only one Latveria gets.
Say...that gives me an idea for some insurance--
YIP! YIP! YIP!
Grrrrrrrreat.
YIP! YIP! YIP! YIP! YIP! YIP!
In order to achieve total silent running, th Ghost Armor store all emissions, which is suppose to mask my odor from even the mos sensitive noses.
...but this is the first time I've worn this suit...
DOOM IS
YIP! YIP! YIP! YIP! YIP! YIP! YIP! YIP! YIP! YIP!
...and clearly some kinks still need to be worked out.
Query: Investigate?
YIP! YIP! YIP! YIP! YIP! YIP! YIP! YIP! YIP! YIP! YIP! YIP! YIP! YIP!
Response: Affirmative.

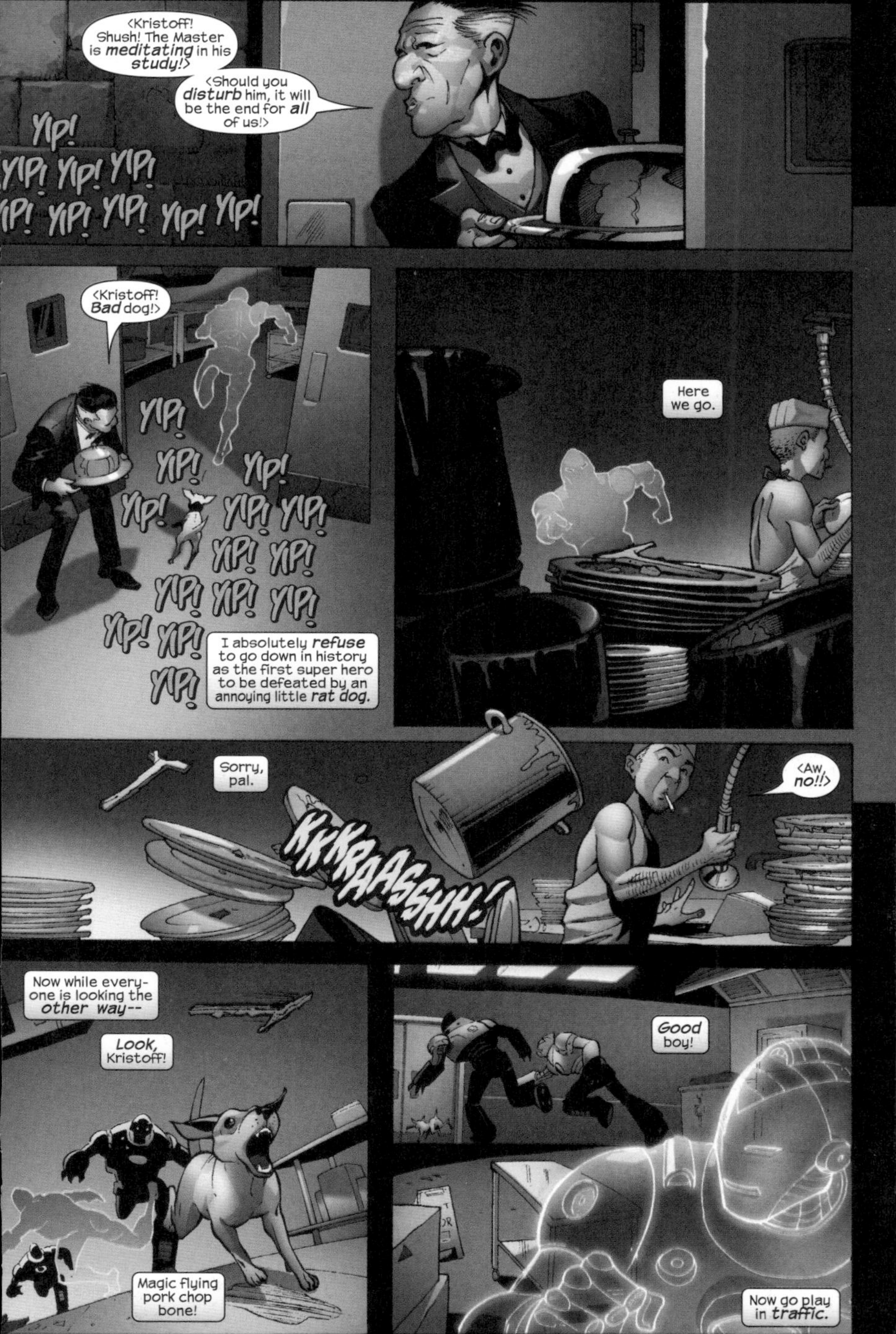

<Kristoff! Shush! The Master is *meditating* in his *study!*>
<Should you *disturb* him, it will be the end for *all* of us!>
YIP! YIP! YIP! YIP! YIP! YIP! YIP! YIP! YIP!
<Kristoff! *Bad* dog!>
YIP! YIP! YIP! YIP! YIP! YIP! YIP! YIP! YIP! YIP! YIP! YIP! YIP! YIP!
I absolutely *refuse* to go down in history as the first super hero to be defeated by an annoying little *rat dog.*
Here we go.
Sorry, pal.
KKKRAASSHH!
<Aw, *no!!*>
Now while every-one is looking the *other way--*
Look, Kristoff!
Magic flying pork chop bone!
Good boy!
Now go play in *traffic.*

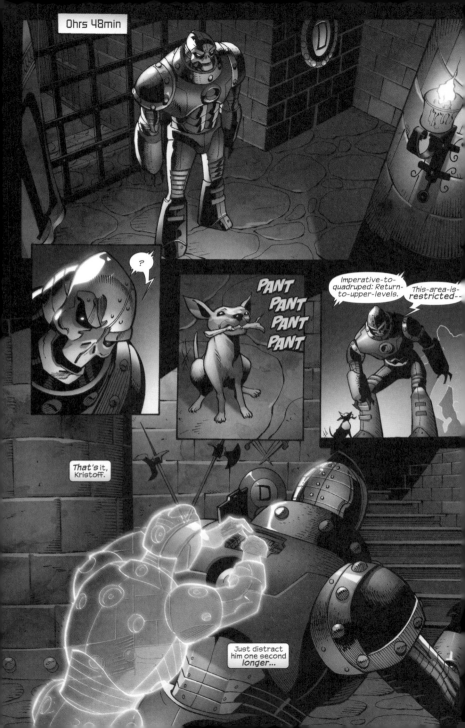

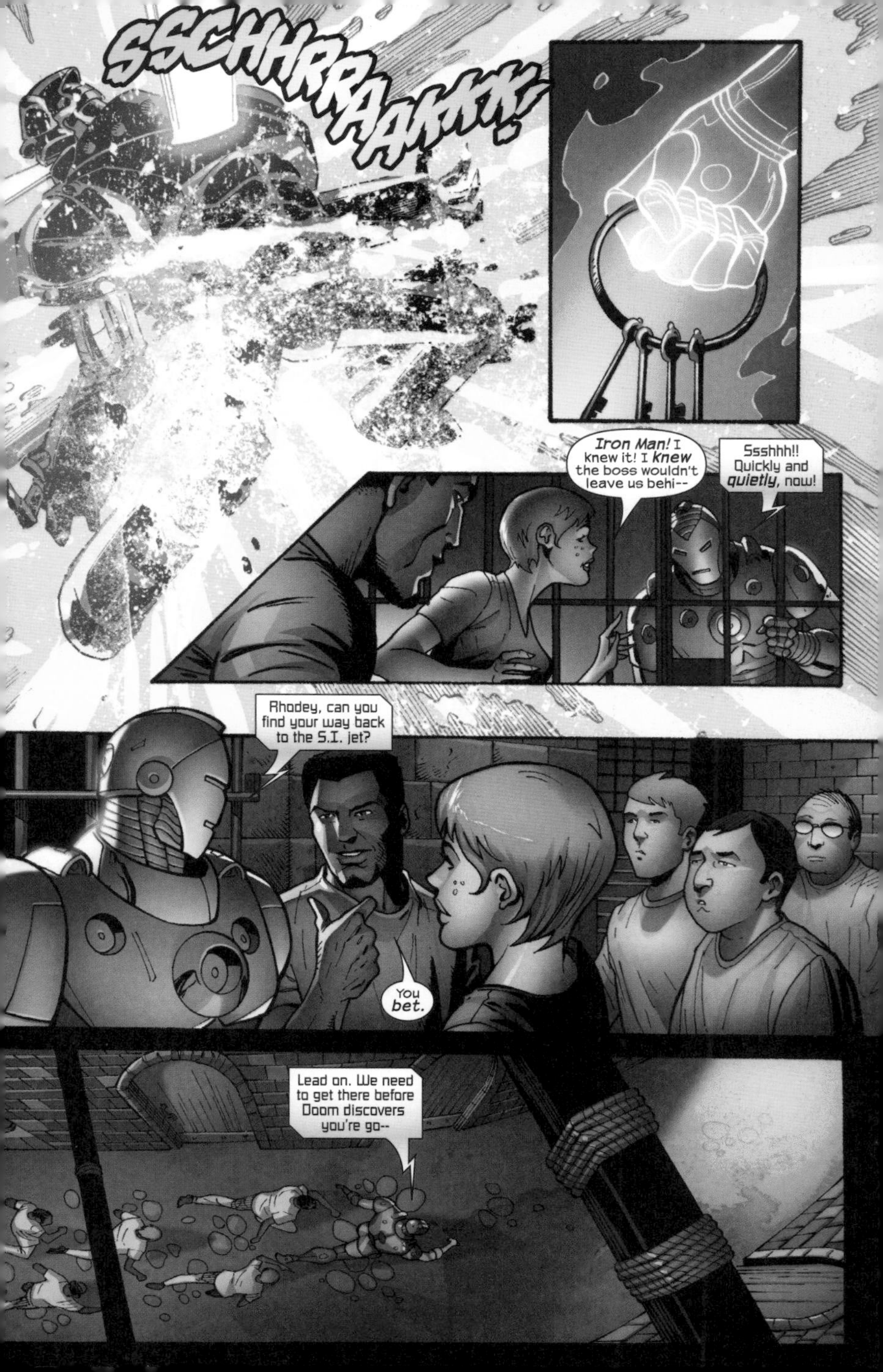
SSCHHRRAAKKK!
Iron Man! I knew it! I knew the boss wouldn't leave us behi--
Ssshhh!! Quickly and quietly, now!
Rhodey, can you find your way back to the S.I. jet?
You bet.
Lead on. We need to get there before Doom discovers you're go--

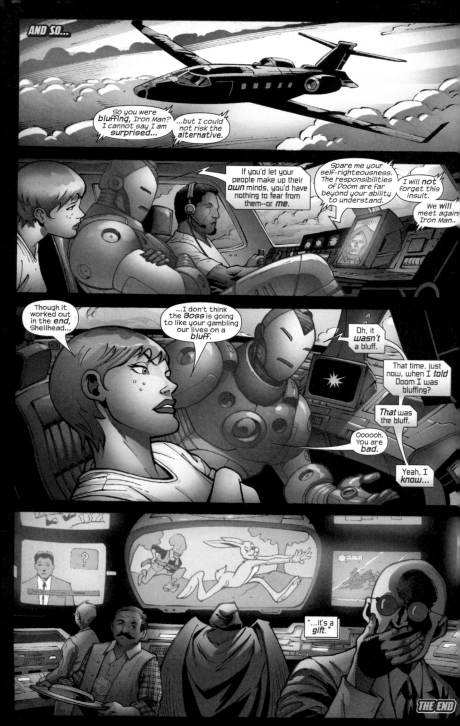

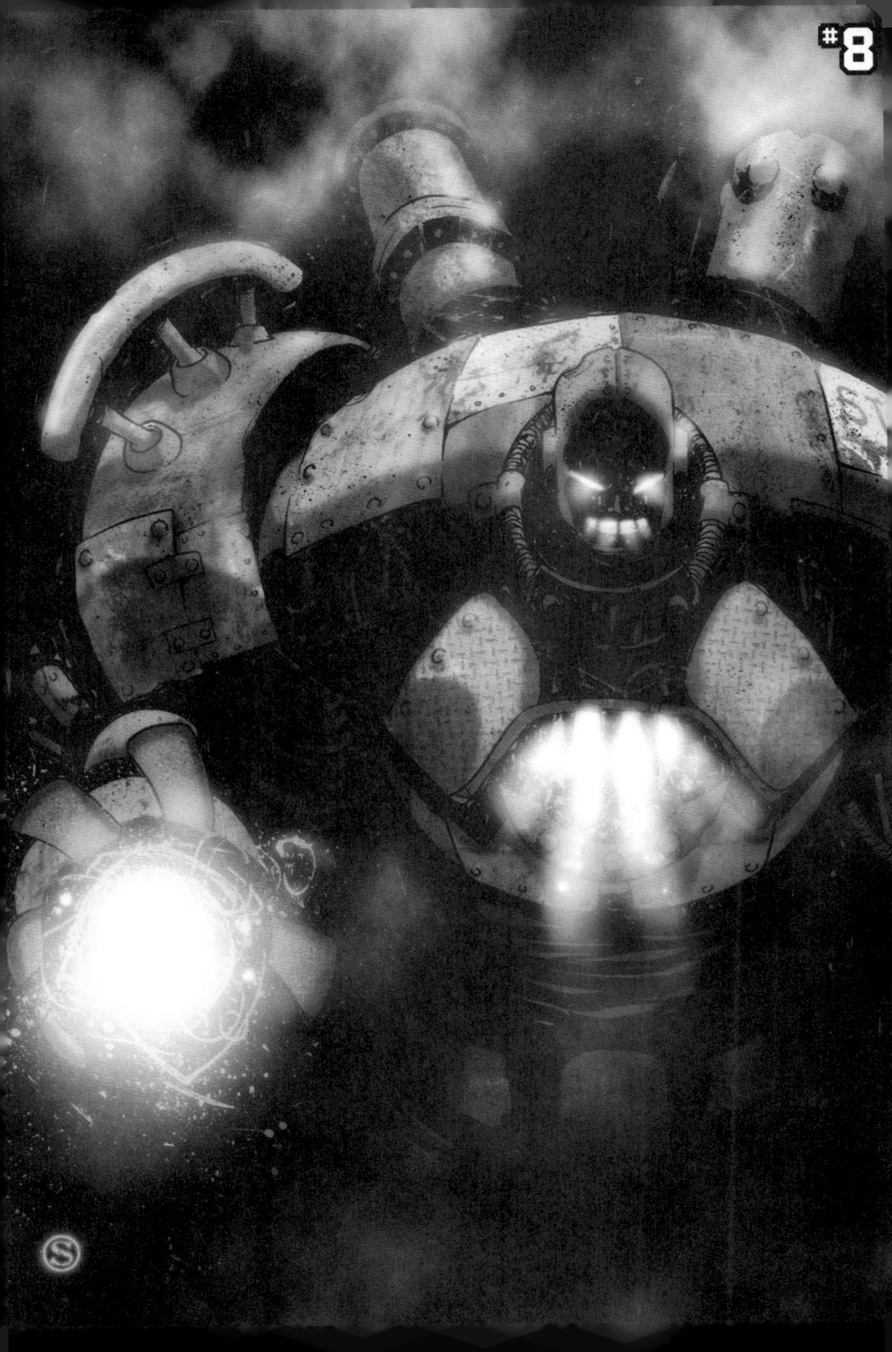
#8

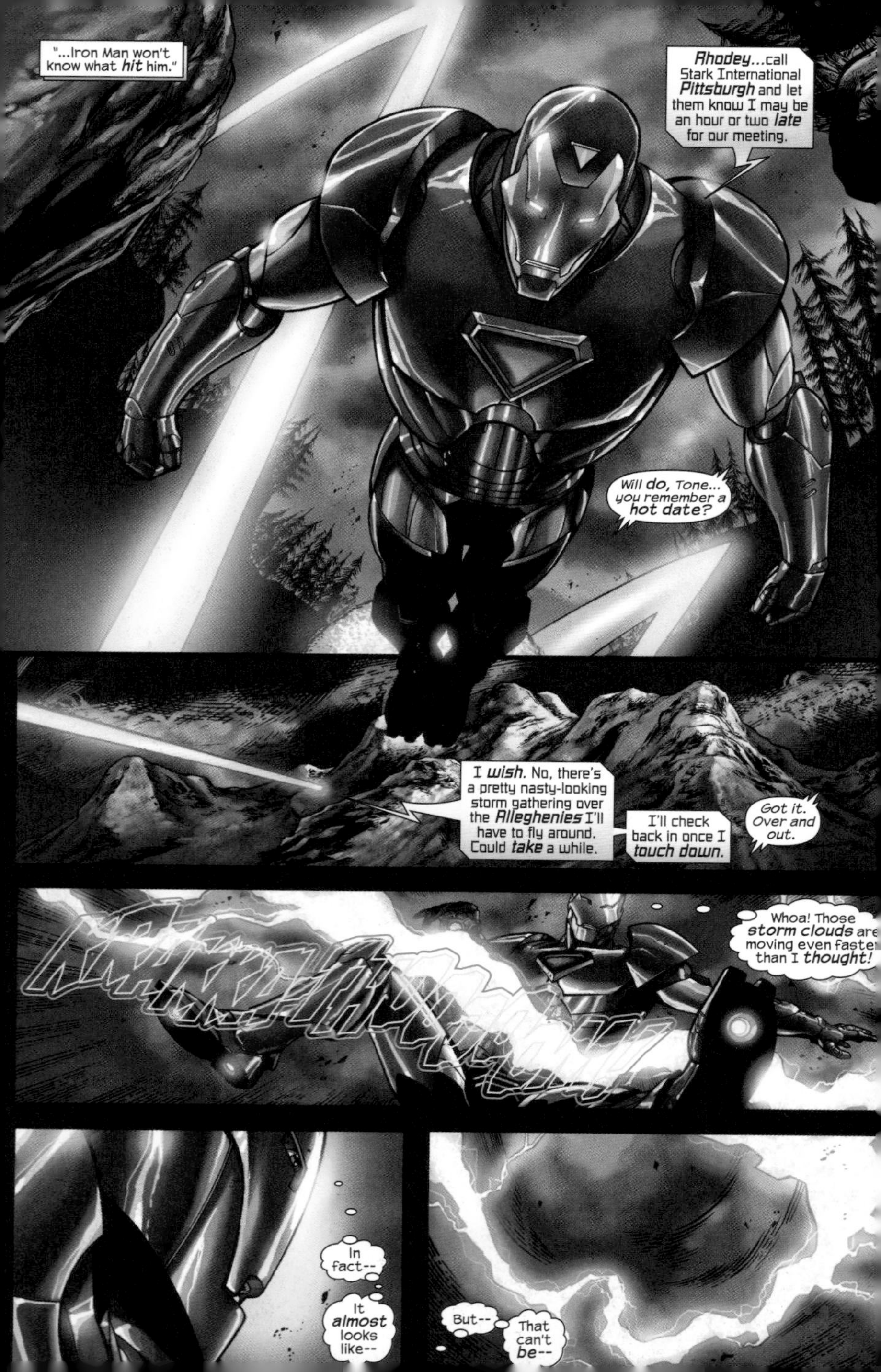

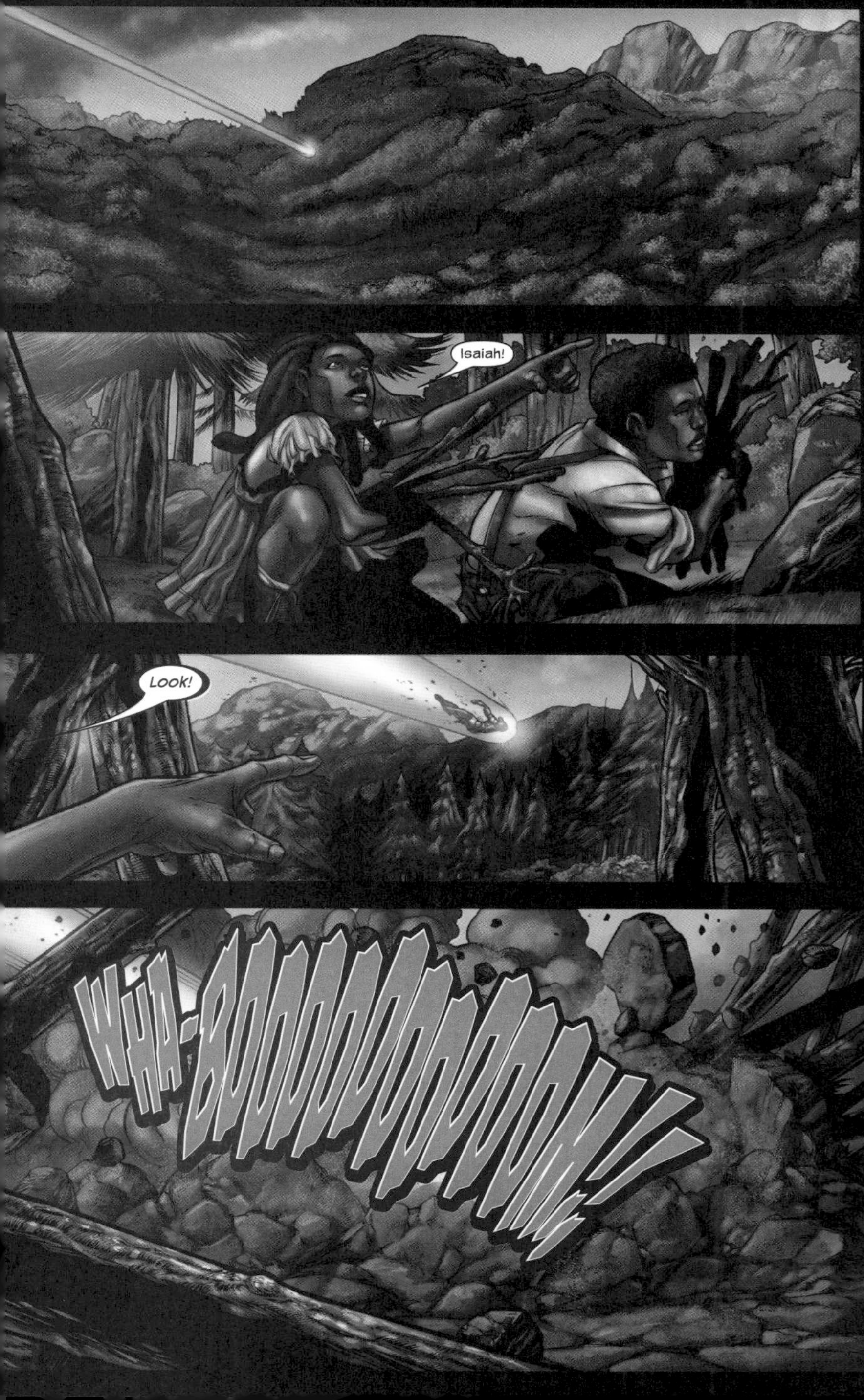
Isaiah!
Look!
WHA-BOOOOOOOOOOM!!

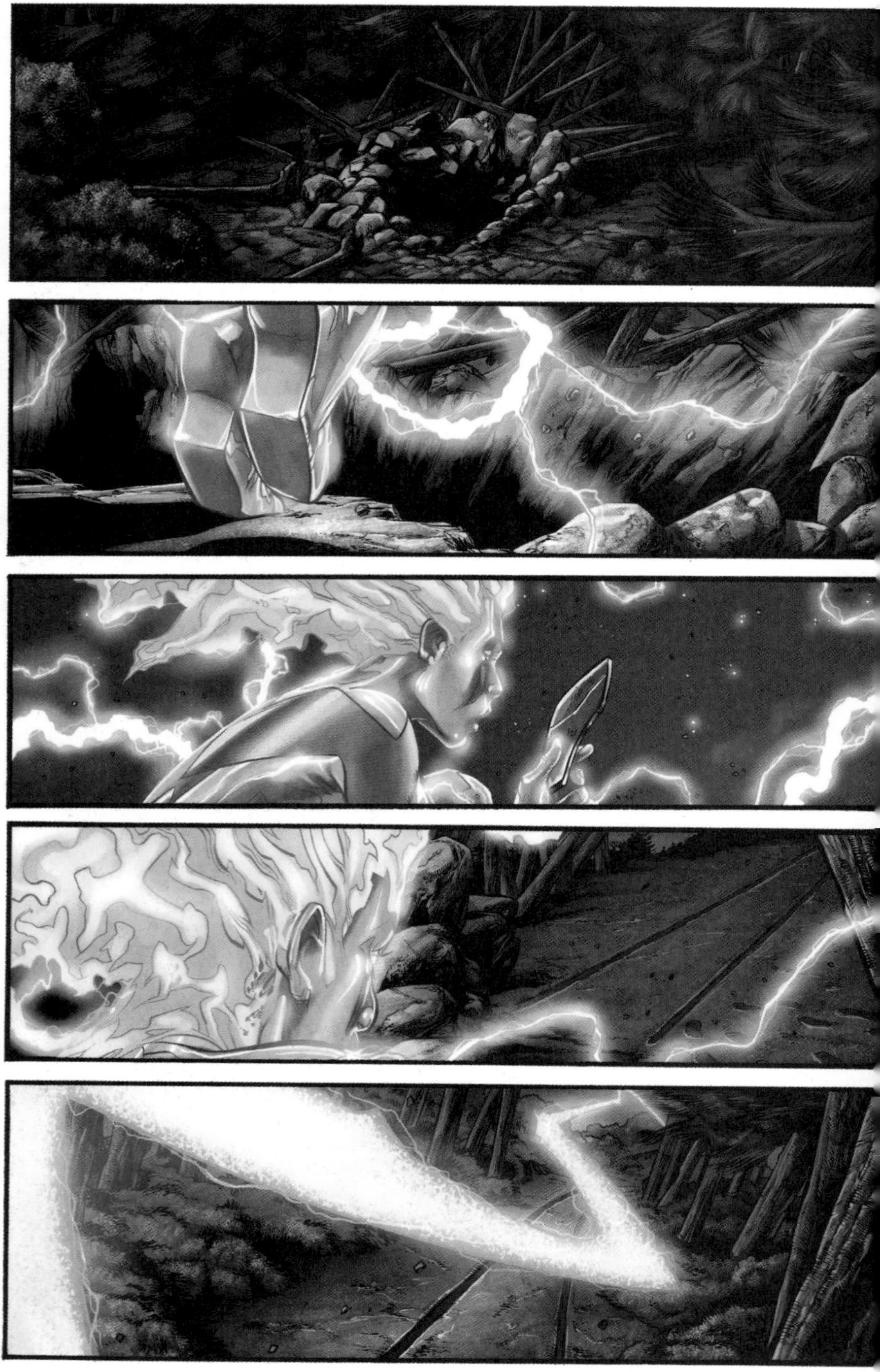

END.